GW00372302

AND THEN I MET JANE

Chapter 1: Betrayal

Nikki didn't feel the bump of the plane as it landed on the tarmac at Alicante Airport, her face leaning against the cool glass of the window. Her mind was still back in England, replaying the events of the night before.

She needed to get away, take some time, lick her wounds and prepare for the awkward questions she knew her father would ask about her just upping and leaving the way she did.

The sun blazing and the birds singing had Nikki's heart feeling light, content even. The pressure of their jobs had caused her and Michael to go through a rough patch, so taking the afternoon off, she intended to ease the tension between them with a homemade lunch, a chilled bottle of wine, and some good old-fashioned love-making for dessert.

Stepping out of her car, she stood looking at the beautifully renovated home she and Michael had worked so hard together in getting just right. A large French Provincial style house, with huge windows. Those belonging to the front bedrooms each had a balcony encased in black wrought iron, the staircase semi-circular white marble, with two marble columns either side. The whole house was painted white, but was far from clinical-looking and, instead, was inviting and welcoming.

Humming softly, she laid her bags of groceries on the floor and rummaged about in her hand bag for her door key. She smiled to herself as she recalled Michael complaining that she had everything in her bag except the kitchen sink. Finding her bunch of keys, she unlocked the freshly painted white front door and stepped into the luxury of her hallway.

The hallway was large, with lofty ceilings, yet still offered a cosy welcome to visitors. The walls, painted in antique white, and the peacock green carpet she had chosen was soft and deeply pilled underfoot. It ran through the hall up the huge staircase and along the landing above. Michael had wanted marble throughout, but Nikki felt that the softness of the carpet beneath one's feet was a lot cosier than cold hard floors. With some gentle coaxing, Michael had relented. Everyone who entered marvelled at how warm and inviting their home looked. The hall was finished with a large French side cabinet, and an easy chair also in peacock green, a few small sunshine-filled paintings and an oversized mirror completed the décor.

Slipping off her kitten-heeled office shoes, Nikki curled her feet into the carpet and sighed a deep sigh. She loved nothing more than walking around in bare feet. Tossing her keys onto the side cabinet, she carried the groceries into the open plan kitchen and placed them onto the shiny black work surfaces, calling Michael's name as she did so.

"Michael," she called, as she walked through the kitchen into the dining area, one of her favourite rooms in the house. A large white farmer style kitchen, the counters of which were in highly polished black marble, with a large green Aga taking pride of place, the dining area was home to the eight-high-backed roll-armed dining chairs, which framed the large white dining table. A low hanging chandelier provided soft lighting for dinner parties, but the piece da resistance was the double French colonial doors leading directly into the garden. The garden was sheltered from the outside world with fully grown conifers. It boasted a well-manicured lawn following a winding pathway into soft seating areas. Flowers of all types and colours bobbed their heads in the soft breeze planted at intervals in huge raised flower beds, and the soft splash of a water fountain added to the tranquillity, Nikki often sat and had breakfast at the wrought iron table or sat quietly when trying to find solace from the ever-increasing pressure of her father's company of which she was a director.

'Lunch out here today,' she thought as she looked at the clear sky and bright sunshine, which brought her back to Michael. Where was he? He said he was working from home today, and his car was in the drive. "Oh, well. Wherever he is, he couldn't have gone far. It gives me time to shower, get out of this suit and prepare lunch," she said aloud to herself.

Taking one more look out onto the garden, she placed the wine in the fridge and made her way up the stairs to her bedroom, rubbing the nape of her neck and grimacing a little. A shower sounded good right now. Her muscles felt stiff from sitting in front of her computer all morning. There were a lot of changes going on at work and the long days, and sometimes nights, were starting to take their toll. 'Maybe Michael is right,' she thought to herself. 'All work and no play make for a very boring marriage'.

Getting a clean towel from the linen cupboard, Nikki made her way towards her bedroom, forcing herself to shut down all thoughts of work. She reached the door to her room. Grasping the door handle, she came to an abrupt halt as she heard voices coming from inside. The blood drained from her face and her heart thudded against her chest as she heard a female voice, a voice she knew, muffled by the closed door. Thinking she must be hearing things, her body automatically leant closer until her ear was pressed up against the cool wood.

"Oh Michael, can't we just stay here a little longer? I feel so relaxed," she heard the female voice plead.

"No, come on, get up. Nikki will be home in a few hours and she deserves more than finding us in here like this," came Michael's reply.

"Well if you told her like you keep saying you will, then we wouldn't have to keep hiding" came the petulant response.

"I will, I will. I just must find the right time. It's not something you can say over breakfast and a cup of coffee, oh, by the way, I'm leaving you for your best friend," Michael replied impatiently.

"Well if you don't tell her soon, then I will," came the female's response, with a hint of malice in her tone.

Nikki felt as if she had been hit with a sledge hammer. Was this really happening? If she opened the door, would the room be empty? Was her over-worked mind playing tricks on her? Looking down at her hand, numb from gripping tightly on the door handle, she knew the answers to these questions, and with a straightening of her shoulders and a release of the breath she had been holding, she turned the handle, swung open the door and walked inside.

****

 Nikki's thoughts were interrupted by the hustle and bustle of other passengers collecting hand luggage from over-head lockers. Waiting for most of the plane to empty, Nikki sighed, collected her small case and made for the exit.

Even though it was 6pm, the air was still humid, showing the remnants of another hot Spanish day. Glad of the airport noise snapping her out of this afternoon's replays running through her mind, Nikki headed towards the 'Nothing to Declare' sign. Passport control was unusually fast flowing, and she didn't even have any hold luggage to wait for, so Nikki soon found herself outside the airport, raising her hand for a taxi. She was soon safely buckled into the back seat. After giving the address of the apartment to the driver, she slumped back into the chair, exhausted and eyes still heavy from unshed tears. Her mind automatically went back to the scene in her bedroom back in England.

****

As Nikki had entered the bedroom, she took in the dishevelled bedding, the bra and panties strewn across the floor, and Michael's trousers laying where they had dropped in his haste to get out of them, obviously. Slowly, after surveying her surroundings, her eyes came to lay on the ashen face of her husband, his mouth agape, like a fish out of water. The silence was deafening, the ticking of the bedside clock the only noise to be heard. Her feet seemed to be glued to the floor, her hand still on the door handle, the only support she had to keep her standing. It was the woman's voice that broke the silence.

"Nikki," came the barely audible whisper of her name. Nikki's head snapped round to the direction of the voice and her eyes meet those of her best friend. Ashley.
"Nikki I – I," Ashley stammered, "I wasn't expecting you home."
"So, I see," Nikki barely recognised her own voice, and was surprised she was able to speak at all. Ashley's eyes held Nikki's for a few seconds before she looked away, but not before Nikki had noticed not only surprise in Ashley's eyes, but also a hint of what looked like satisfaction.

Michael was busy trying to pull his trousers on, one leg in and hopping around trying to find the other leg. Nikki looked at him now, her husband, her friend, her lover, nearly falling over himself trying to get dressed and all she could think of was how scrawny his legs looked. Once safely into his trousers, Michael headed in Nikki's direction. But, before he reached her, she stilled him with the lift of her hand.

"Get her out of our bedroom," she said, pointing her head towards where Ashley was still covered by a sheet in her bed. "And give her those." She forced through gritted teeth, giving a look of distain at the panties on the floor. With a straight back and a strength, she didn't know she had, she walked towards the bathroom, turning before she closed the door. "And Ashley?" the other woman turned to look at her. "You're fired." With those words, Nikki closed and bolted the bathroom door.

Once inside, Nikki felt her legs give way and the first sob escaped her lips as she slid slowly down the door onto the floor. Placing her head on her knees and wrapping her arms around them, her body shook. The hurt, anger and shock were releasing itself in bone-shaking sobs, and she cried. She cried like she had never cried before, trying to suck in air between each sob. Her lungs burnt with the effort of searching for oxygen. She was going to be sick. Just making it to the toilet on her knees, she threw up, the image of them together causing her to retch until there was nothing left except the pain of her stomach muscles. She rested her head on her arms, not feeling strong enough to make it to the basin to wash the vomit from around her mouth, using the back of her hand instead.

How long she stayed there, she wasn't sure. She was only brought back to reality when she heard the tapping at the bathroom door.

Nikki slowly lifted her head and looked at the door as if she wasn't aware of what it was or where she was. The tapping came again, more persistent this time.

"Nikki, Nikki," Michael's voice called. "Nikki please open the door."

Staying where she was, she rested her head on her arms again. A thumping headache had started, and she was feeing nauseous again.

"Nikki," came Michael's voice, sounding more urgent now. "Are you ok? Open the door, Nikki. If you don't open the door, I will kick it open, Nikki. Please, are you ok?"

'What did he think she had done?' She thought to herself. Slit her wrists? But with the threat of the door being kicked, she called back.

"Is she gone?"

"Yes, she's gone. Just open the door, Nikki, please."

Slowly, she got to her feet. Passing the mirror, she looked at her reflection. Eyes swollen and almost closed from crying so much, face patchy and red, the woman looking back at her didn't look like her at all. With a shaking hand, Nikki slid the bolt and the door was quickly pushed open, there he was, her betrayer, standing just a few inches away. Their eyes locked for just a few seconds before Nikki pushed past him and made her way down the stairs into the kitchen where she sat staring out into the garden that looked so beautiful just a short while ago, but now seemed as forlorn as she felt right now. She recalled the summer weekends spent together, pulling up weeds, laying lawn, planting their favourite flowers, laughing at some silly joke they shared, rolling around the ground like a couple of school kids. This was supposed to be their happy place, where they would raise their children, the garden that they would play in as Michael and her sipped wine and watched them grow. But now that was gone. All gone. The dream they once shared was no more than that – just a dream. The sadness she felt was like a lead blanket that she couldn't move, and tears once more ran down her cheeks, but she quickly brushed them away.

Michael entered the kitchen, shuffling from foot to foot, not sure what to say or where to start. After an uncomfortable silence, Michael walked to the counter and started to spoon coffee into a mug. Nikki studied his back. A back she had run her hands over many times. A back she had often laid her head on while he was still sleeping. Picturing Ashley's hands following the contours of his body, she felt the bile rise in the back of her throat and quickly diverted her gaze back to the garden.

The silence was broken by the coffee being placed in front of her.
"Drink this. I've put a little whisky in there."
Nikki grasped the mug between her hands, concentrating on the dark liquid in the cup. She didn't want to look up and didn't want to investigate Michael's eyes, scared of what she may see there. She heard the scrape of the chair as Michael took a seat opposite her. Taking a sip of the coffee, she felt the hot liquid burn the back of her throat. She was grateful

for the hit of whisky that then followed it. She needed something to calm her jangled nerves.

Nikki jumped a little when Michael called her name. "Nikki, look at me, please, I need to explain."

Nikki slowly looked up from the coffee mug, not quite meeting Michael's gaze. Instead, her eyes came to rest on his Adam's apple, and she saw the way it moved up and down as he swallowed before continuing.

"Please Nikki, say something, scream, shout, throw something at me. I can't bare this silence. We need to talk. You need to let me explain."

Finding her voice, she replied, "Explain? Explain how you been fucking my PA? Fucking my best friend, in our bed? You want to explain that to me?" The venom she spat with each word surprised her. She was usually so calm, and this feeling was alien to her. This whole scenario felt like a bad dream and she was praying that she would wake up soon.

Michael was obviously taken aback by the tone in her voice. The usually relaxed, easily cajoled woman he was used to seemed to have been taken over by a snarling tiger ready to pounce.

He didn't know how to handle this Nikki.

Nikki noticed his Adam's apple dancing as he swallowed, thinking of what to say next to her. She moved her gaze to the midnight shadow on his chin, to the strong, slightly wide nose she had often kissed, and then their eyes met. She could see her tone had startled him as it had her, and she took some comfort in knowing that he was disconcerted. What did he think she was going to do? Lay on the floor like some wounded animal howling? No. She wouldn't give him the satisfaction in knowing that's just what she felt like doing right now.

"I—I am so sorry Nikki, sorry you found us..." He gestured to the stairs. "It's not serious," he continued, "I mean, I don't love her Nikki. It's just we—we were going through a tough time, and she was there to talk to. And, well, I needed someone Nikki. We haven't made love in weeks. You're always so tired, and she was just there. I tried to break it off, I really did, but...." His voice trailed off as he looked across the table. Nikki was staring at him like she didn't know him, like he was a stranger. This wasn't good. Not good at all. This wasn't the way it was supposed to go.

Nikki firmly shook her head. "So, this is my fault? This is what you're telling me? That's your explanation? That this is all my fault because I've been too tired to make love?"

"No that's not what I meant. It wasn't your fault Nikki. This is all mine. Please, I don't want you to feel like you're to blame. This is all my fault."
Nikki laughed out loud, "Oh Michael, I don't blame myself! I never stripped you both and forced you into bed together." I've been working my arse off, trying to put a home together for us – for our children." Nikki felt the tears well up again. "And your contribution to this was fucking my best friend. Your arrogant bastard!" she screamed.

Chapter 2: Taking Time

"The Gemelos," the taxi driver said. Nikki looked at him, her mind still back in England, not quiet registering where she was. "The Gemelos" the taxi driver repeated impatiently. Nikki shook herself back to the present and looked out the window at the apartments. Getting out of the taxi, she retrieved her bag from the boot of the car, paying her fare and tipping the driver for his time. He smiled and, with a quick adios, he was gone.

Standing for a while, getting her bearings, Nikki looked up at the sign above the apartments. She could have afforded any of the five-star hotels but didn't want to bump into the many people she knew holidayed here. She wanted anonymity. A place where she didn't have to make small talk over expensive cocktails She wanted space, and time to sort out where she went from here. What to do next, to feel the pain and heal her wounds. She felt lost. Her life so far was about the family business, Michael and their future together, confident in knowing where life was taking her. Now she didn't know who she was, she needed to find herself to plan a new life and this scared her. She was still raw from the ending of her marriage, and she couldn't see past the here and now, let alone consider the future.

Entering the cool foyer, she went to reception and checked into her apartment. Hot, tired and weary, she stepped into the lift as instructed by the receptionist and pushed the button for the 7th floor.

"Hold the door," she heard a voice call. Hitting the door 'open' button, Nikki was greeted by a whirl of blonde hair and perfume. "Thanks," the short, t-shirt-clad woman said." These lifts can take ages."

Nikki nodded her head and rested her back against the lift wall. Suitcase in front of her, she kept her eyes down, not wanting to invite any conversation, not that this seemed to make a difference to the young woman who had invaded the small confines of the elevator.

"You just arrived?" The woman asked. Without waiting for a reply, she went on, "I'm Jane. You will love the apartments. Real spacious, with a good-sized balcony. How long you here for?"

Nikki lifted her eyes and looked directly into the soft blue eyes of the whirlwind standing in front of her. She took in the sun- bleached shoulder length hair, make up-free face, a small stub nose and the most beautifully shaped lips she had ever seen on a woman.

"A week, two weeks"? Jane continued.

Nikki realised she hadn't answered and had just been staring, feeling her cheeks flush a little. "Err, I'm not sure," she replied hastily.

"Ah, just needed a quick getaway?" Jane replied, nodding her head, smiling.

"I never said that…" Nikki responded with an indignant tone to her voice and her jaw set into a determined 'don't you dare presume you know me' rigidity.

But before anymore could be said, the elevator came to a halt on the 7th floor, and Nikki pushed past Jane.

With a parting look over her shoulder, Nikki explained, "I came here to be left alone".

As Nikki made her way along the corridor to her apartment, she heard Jane comment, "Then you came to the wrong place." With that, the lift door closed, and she was once again alone.

Once inside the apartment, Nikki took in her surroundings. There was a large living space with two sofas, a separate, albeit small, kitchen area, and, off to the side, a double bedroom. A little further down the corridor, there was a bathroom with a shower and toilet. Walking towards the balcony, she opened the orange curtains then opened the door. She had a pool view. Leaning over the balcony, she took in sun loungers filled with women in scant bikinis and men in speedos, even at this hour!

There was a pool side bar with a few of the older guests sitting on stools having coffee or their favourite tipple. She felt safe, she knew no one, and no one knew her. She was just another face in the crowd. She felt invisible, and that's just what she wanted to be until she figured out what to do next. She needed to allow the events of the past few hours to unravel in her mind, to examine her life that remained, and to take steps towards making a life on her own – a divorced 34-year-old woman not sure of who she was or where she was going anymore.

Sighing a deep sigh, Nikki went back inside. She took some underwear, shorts and T-shirt from her case and headed for the shower. Feeling a little better and refreshed, she made her way to the bedroom and, with the sound of children playing and splashing in the pool, she fell into a deep, dreamless sleep.

Awaking with a start, she reached out to Michael, only to find an empty place beside her. It took Nikki a few minutes to realise where she was. She felt an overwhelming sense of loneliness and desolation. Hot tears burning her eyes, she forced herself to get up. She couldn't allow the depression that loomed to take over, she needed to lick her wounds, but she also needed to feel the sun on her skin and breathe fresh air into her lungs.

Needing a strong coffee, Nikki ventured to the little café she had noticed next door to her apartment on the evening she had arrived. Making a mental note to find the local supermarket to stock up on essentials, she made for the stairs, not wanting to partake in small talk with any of the other guests who may be using the lifts. And, for a reason she didn't quite understand, she was still feeling a little rankled about that Jane woman she had met yesterday.

Weaving her way through the many guests staying at The Gemelos, she made her way out into the hot sunshine, instantly regretting not wearing a hat and feeling the heat beating down on her head. She turned left and came upon the Union Jack café. Taking a seat in the shade, Nikki ordered her first coffee of the day. She could feel it was going to be a hot one, her light dress clinging to her damp body. Getting out her shopping list, she added 'sun cream', then leaned back in her chair and, under the privacy of her sunglasses, surveyed her surroundings and the mill of people walking past.

She liked this feeling of anonymity as she sat here at the table sipping her coffee, she looked up as she heard giggling and saw the same blonde girl from the lift leaning against a wall, laughing with a group of people. Swigging water from a bottle, the woman's shorts were showing off her tanned legs. She looked so relaxed and, just for a moment, Nikki felt a pang of jealousy.

Jane looked like she didn't have a care in the world – unlike Nikki, who felt like she had the weight of the world on her shoulders, trying to figure out how to disentangle herself from this marriage that she knew was over. Regardless of how many times Michael said sorry or that they could start afresh, it wouldn't make a difference. She wished she had the same freedom as the woman she was quietly surveying, with her sun-bleached hair, full lips and shining blue eyes. Nikki physically shook herself. What the hell was she doing? Why was she mapping out this woman's features in her mind? She felt herself blush a little as she paid her bill and made her way back through the hotel foyer to the pool area, her shopping trip forgotten.

"Must be this sun frazzling my brain," she muttered to herself, as she found a sunbed, took off her dress to reveal a figure hugging white bikini, and laid down, keeping her sunglasses on as a barrier to the rest of the guests – or so she thought.

"Hi!"

Nikki lifted her glasses to see Jane sitting on the sunbed next to hers

"Hi," Nikki replied with a quick smile and then covered her eyes again to ward off any further conversation.

"So, you been laying here all morning?" Jane continued, oblivious to the 'leave me alone' posture Nikki had resumed. Sighing and lifting her sun glasses onto her head, Nikki replied, "Not all day, no. I went for coffee and then came here to get some time alone."

Again, Jane didn't take the hint, and continued, "You need to put some cream on that skin of yours. It's already starting to go red", following her gaze, Nikki could see the slight change in her skin colour across her chest.

"Well, I'm going inside now, anyway." Nikki replied. And, with that, she stood, gathered her belongings and started to walk away.

"Always running off, aren't ya?" She heard Jane say. Spinning back around, Nikki could barely contain her snarl as she replied, "Don't presume you know me. Maybe you should learn a little about space and, next time, give me some".

Jane didn't flinch from the look of anger in Nikki's eyes but, instead, held her gaze. Nikki was the first to look away, but not before seeing something akin to desire in Jane's eyes. She must be imagining things. This sun was getting to her and she was still mentally exhausted from everything that had happened in the past few days.

"Just, please, respect my privacy." Nikki retorted, turning on her heel and walking away.

Once back in her apartment, she realised she hadn't got a single thing she needed from the store. She would have to go out again.

'Blast that woman,' Nikki thought, throwing her bag on the bed. 'Well, I'm going to take a shower first,' she thought. The area of skin Jane had mentioned earlier started to feel sore. A strange feeling hit Nikki's tummy as she remembered the look in Jane's eyes before physically shaking herself again and heading for the shower.

Her phone was ringing when she entered the living area, picking it up and walking onto the balcony her heart sank as she heard Michael's voice.

"Hello, hello Nikki, are you there?"

She paused for a while before answering, "Michael, I told you not to contact me, I need time to think and be on my own."

"I know, I know, but I miss you. I'm worried about you. Where are you? Let me come and meet you – we need to talk."

The whining tone to Michael's voice grated on her and she replied maybe a little more vehemently than need be.

"This isn't all about you, Michael. You are so bloody selfish! I have asked you to give me some time. I think, after all that's happened, you could at least allow me that"

"And I'm trying, Nikki, really, I am, but I miss you so much. I want to sort out this mess that I've made."

"And I need time to sort out the mess in my head," explained Nikki. "I will contact you when I know where I'm going Michael – until then, give me the space I need."

Nikki hung up the phone and texted her dad, letting him know that she was fine but that she just needed a break and would contact him soon. Ending her text with 'I love you' and a kiss, her phone bleeped almost as soon as the message was sent.

'I love you too Nikki,' came her dad's response. 'I am here for you whenever you are ready to talk, whatever it is sweetheart we can sort it out.'

The soft caring words from her father brought tears to her eyes. Blinking them back, she decided she was hungry, and the low growl in her tummy confirmed this. So, pulling on shorts and a t-shirt, she ventured out of her apartment for the second time that day.

****

Michael looked at the phone as if it was alien to him. She hung up on him! He put the phone down in disbelief. Who the hell did she think she was, treating him like that? He was her husband.

All thoughts of his infidelity disappeared as his guilt turned to anger. The small vein in his forehead pulsed as anger and frustration seeped through his body and mind. Reaching for the half empty whisky bottle on the table in front of him, he refilled his tumbler. He had been drinking heavily since Nikki left, and it was the only comfort he had.

'She will learn...' he said aloud, taking a large gulp from the glass. She belonged to him. Just give her a little more time to deal with her 'lady tantrum' she was having and then she would be back. He knew her. He knew what she most wanted in the world. He smiled to himself as he took another drink from the glass, and he decided that he would facilitate that want. He would make her pregnant. Then all thoughts of that silly day with Ashley would vanish, and things would go back to where they were before – only better.

Getting up from the chair, a little unsteady on his feet, he walked towards the door. He needed to get some much-needed sleep before going to the office tomorrow. Lifting the bottle of whisky from the table, feeling better now he had a plan, he made his way upstairs and into the bedroom. Clothes still on, he laid spread eagle across the bed and stayed there until morning.

****

Finding a seat away from the crowd, Nikki sat at a table in the Union Jack. Taking off her sun hat, she shook her auburn hair. It framed her pretty face in a shower of waves. She hated her wavy hair, thinking it too unruly, always finding its way out of any type of bun or other hairstyle she tried. She had seemed to attract some attention from a few guys on another table who were staring at her and whispering. She was used to male attention but always had Michael to shield her from over enthusiastic guys. She kept her eyes fixed firmly on the menu in front of her and hoped that their attention would soon be caught elsewhere. But this was not to be the case.

"Hi." She heard a male voice loaded with a Spanish accent say.

"Hello," Nikki replied, keeping her eyes on the menu, hoping that the guy would get the hint and leave.

"Would you mind if I sat here?" The guy asked, ignoring her blatant lack of enthusiasm.

"I would prefer it if you didn't," Nikki started, but the guy had dragged out the chair and sat down opposite her.

"May I suggest the seafood paella? It is, how you say, delicioso." He continued, kissing his fingers in the traditional Spanish way.

"Oh, how rude of me, let me introduce myself. I am Mateo." He held out his hand across the table, but Nikki ignored the gesture.

"I'm Nikki, but, if you don't mind – erm – Mateo, I would prefer to eat alone."

"But why would a pretty woman like you dine alone?" He continued.

Nikki looked up from her menu. Mateo was dark, very attractive, laid back and relaxed, as if he had practiced this line many a time.

"I just do not feel like any conversation this evening. I really would like to be alone."

Nikki saw the challenge in Mateo's eyes. She could tell he wasn't used to being refused.

"Then why you shake your lovely hair and look in my direction?" He went to touch Nikki's hair and she pushed herself back, scrapping her chair along the floor as she did so, causing people to look in her direction. She saw the gleam of annoyance in Mateo's eyes and went to get up and leave, rather than give this man anymore of her time, when she heard a familiar voice.

"I think the lady asked to be left alone," she heard Jane say in a quiet yet 'don't mess with me' kind of voice.

"It's fine, I'm no longer hungry," Nikki replied, starting to stand.

"No, sit and enjoy a meal. This gentleman is just about to leave." Jane tilted her head slightly, looking Mateo up and down with a slight look of disgust on her face.

"Who the hell you think you are? You stupid English bitch." Mateo stood to his full height, towering above Jane... She didn't flinch. Instead, she started a tirade of Spanish towards him, attracting the attention of the not-so-small barman.

"There is a problem, Jane?" The barman asked, obviously a

friend of hers.

"No, I don't think so, Samuel, this gentleman," she said with a slight snarl to her voice "Is just about to leave."

Mateo edged a little closer to Jane. The rage he was feeling showed on his face.

"You heard the lady." Samuel stepped between the two, matching Mateo's height evenly, but standing much broader than him. "Unless you need help finding the door, of course." Samuel's voice was low and menacing.

Mateo took a step back, and then gave a fake laugh. "You want them both?" He gestured with a wave of his hand. "Be my guest."

After a few Spanish remarks under his breath, Mateo turned on his heel and left the restaurant.

"I am sorry this man bothered you," Samuel turned his attention to Nikki, "Please, if he bothers you anymore, just come and get me," he said in perfect English but a deep Spanish accent. He offered his hand to Nikki and said, "My name is Samuel. I am here most days. Now please let me take your order."

Nikki took the outstretched hand and smiled warmly.

"Thank you," she replied, ordering a toasted sandwich with some coffee, although she really didn't feel hungry anymore.

As Samuel turned away to get her order, Nikki turned towards Jane.

"Thank you," she repeated.

"No problem. You get some like that," Jane gestured with her thumb to the restaurant door. "Enjoy your meal. I'm off to get some much-needed rest."

With that, Jane, with her incredible smile, was gone.

Nikki sat and ate her sandwich, not really tasting it. She ought to buy Jane a bottle of wine or something for coming to her rescue. She really couldn't be dealing with that guy right now and he had shown no signs of leaving her alone at her own request. Drinking the last of her coffee, she made her way to the small supermarket just across the road, wondering if Jane preferred red or white and deciding to get both just in case.

Jane had taken a shower and was now sitting on her balcony, towel drying her hair. She was thinking about the smile that Nikki had given Samuel. A smile that completely transformed her already beautiful face but didn't quite reach her eyes that were masking a hurt she was feeling. Jane wondered what or who it was that had caused that hurt, but then shook her head. No getting involved with pretty ladies with baggage, she told herself out loud, never mind how much she wanted to kiss Nikki's lips. The thought of her mouth on Nikki's sent a stirring in her tummy that went further down, causing a slight dampness.

'No,' she chastised herself out loud and proceeded to put on the kettle to pull her mind away from the path it was heading. Just about to walk into the small kitchenette, Jane heard a knock at the door, sighing heavily as she really didn't want visitors, she opened the door slightly to see who was there.

Nikki stood in the apartment door way looking slightly uncomfortable.

"Hi," Nikki said, "I hope I'm not disturbing you or anything, but I wanted to say thank you properly so bought these." Holding out both hands, she asked, "Red or white?"

Jane stood back and motioned for Nikki to come inside. After a few seconds of hesitation, Nikki accepted the invitation and walked into an apartment much the same as hers.

"I really didn't mean to disturb you. I just wanted to thank you properly for saving me today," Nikki smiled, still feeling a little uncomfortable but not quite knowing why. She held the two bottles in front of her while looking everywhere else except at Jane.

"You didn't have to buy me wine," Jane replied. "It's one of my forties, rescuing damsels in distress." Jane smiled, "But I will have a glass of red, if you join me."

"Oh, I was just going to have an early night," Nikki started to say.

"You wouldn't force a girl to drink alone, would you?" Jane could see that Nikki seemed on edge but wanted her to stay a while. There was something about this woman that intrigued her. She wanted to get to know her a little better. She wanted to find out what or who had caused the pain in her eyes.

"OK, but just a small glass. Wine tends to go straight to my head," Nikki replied.

Jane gestured to the sofa for Nikki to sit down and went to fetch two glasses. Sitting on the edge of the sofa, picking imaginary fluff from her clothing, Nikki could not fathom out why she felt so nervous. She had had many a glass of wine with female company, but she felt self-conscious of how she looked. She mentally chided herself. What the hell was wrong with her?

Jane stood in front of her holding out a glass of red wine. Nikki took the glass and gulped a mouthful down, feeling a shock of electricity as their hands touched slightly.
'For God's sake,' she thought to herself, 'Get a grip.'
Jane didn't seem to notice and planted herself on the coffee table facing Nikki.

"Cheers," Jane smiled, taking a sip from her glass.
"Cheers," Nikki replied, doing the same. For a few minutes, there was an awkward silence until Nikki asked, "So, you work here? In Benidorm, I mean?"
Jane took another sip of her wine before replying. "Yes, for the past two years. I do a bit of bar work; sometimes help in the restaurant you were at today… I came here to get away from life for a bit, fell in love with the place and haven't been home since. And you?" She asked, "Why are you here in Benidorm alone?"

Nikki looked down at her glass. Did she really finish her wine? She didn't remember drinking it all. Jane offered her the bottle and she gratefully poured herself another glass.
"I just needed some alone time," Nikki replied. "I have a few things I need to sort out which I couldn't do in England."
Jane nodded her head, "And you don't want to talk about it, right?"
"No not really," Nikki replied, "I haven't even sorted things

out in my head, let alone put them into words!" She laughed half-heartedly.

Jane could see the hurt in Nikki's eyes so didn't want to press the subject. She changed the direction of the conversation. "So, is this your first time in Benidorm?"

Nikki shook her head, "No I used to holiday here with my parents when I was a kid, and still come back as often as I can, but it's the first time I've stayed at The Gemelos."

"Would you like some more wine?" Jane asked.

Nikki looked at her glass and realised it was once again empty. "No, no, thank you. I've already had one glass too many and it goes straight to my head. I'd better go."

Jane would have liked her to stay longer but stood and thanked her again for the wine.

"Maybe you would allow me to buy you a drink at the bar sometime?" Jane said, hoping she could spend more time in this woman's company.

"Maybe," Nikki returned as she headed for the door. "But I'm not very good company at the moment."

"Well maybe a bit of socialising will make you feel better," Jane smiled.

Nikki smiled back, "Goodnight, Jane, and thanks again for today."

She closed the door quietly behind her, leaving Jane staring at the door for a few minutes, not liking the silence of the apartment that she had always enjoyed before. Sighing, Jane turned and made her way to the bedroom.

Nikki entered her apartment and switched on the kettle. After eating so little tonight, she felt slightly light-headed after the wine. Leaning against the counter, she wondered what it was that made her feel awkward in Jane's company. She didn't want to be around anyone right now but, for some reason, found herself thinking that she would quite like that drink in the bar. Making her coffee, she took it with her to her bedroom, promising herself a shower in the morning. That night, she dreamed of hands touching her. Not rough, masculine hands but soft feminine ones caressing her body, and gentle sweet lips kissing hers. In her sleep, she smiled and moaned softly.

Nikki rose early and made a call to her father. Hearing his deep voice on the end of the line made her miss him more.
"Hi, Dad."
"Nikki, darling, how are you? Are you eating properly, are you…"
Nikki stopped him mid-flow, "Dad, Dad, I'm fine. Stop worrying!"
"It's my job to worry about you. You're my little girl," her father laughed gently. Then, on a more serious note, said, "Are you sure you're OK, Nick? Michael's walking around like a bear with a sore head, and you not wanting him knowing where you are… What's going on Nikki? Whatever it is, you know you can tell me."
"I know, Dad, and I will tell you everything, I promise. But please just give me a little more time. I need to sort some things out in my head, then we can sit down and talk."

"Ok darling, but please don't stay away too long. I miss my little girl."

Reassuring her father that she would be home soon and promising him once again that she was eating properly, she ended the call, feeling a little better from hearing her father's voice.

Nikki's father wasn't a stupid man. He knew there had been trouble in paradise. It's the only reason that made any sense of his daughter's quick getaway. It wasn't like her to up and leave like that, and Michael's dishevelled appearances in the office these last few days were testament that all was not well. He was sure they would sort it out. Nikki loved the bones of Michael, but somewhere in the back of his mind was that niggle that wouldn't go away. He loved his daughter dearly, and just wanted her to be happy. If Michael was making her unhappy, he would have plenty to say to him. Nikki was the most important person in his life and always would be.

Chapter 3: A softer touch

Hearing the splash of the water from the pool below and the laughter of children, Nikki rested her arms on the balcony and smiled at the fun they seemed to be having. Looking over the sunbeds, her eyes came to rest on a figure she knew. Jane was stretched out on the sunbed, shades covering her eyes, her brown body glistening in the sun. Nikki felt her cheeks turn red as she remembered her dream last night. The feeling of the female's hands over her body, the dampness between her legs when she woke this morning. Why the hell was she dreaming of Jane making love to her? Was the shock she had suffered witnessing Michael and his whore together making her lose her mind?

She had never experienced a dream like that before. She could still remember the taste of those lips. The feel of her hands massaging her breasts... Suddenly Nikki heard her name called, snapping her back to reality, and noticed Jane waving at her from beside the pool. She felt her cheeks burn brighter, thankful that she was far enough away for Jane not to see and gave a wave back.

Jane was motioning for her to come down, and Nikki indicated 10 minutes with her fingers, before heading for the shower. She wondered why she had that funny feeling in her tummy at the prospect of seeing Jane again, convincing herself that it was the fact that Jane had helped her the night before, and that socialising was probably good for her. She showered in record time and headed down to the pool in a little peach two peace, knowing that she looked good, but not knowing why she cared.

Jane watched her approach from beneath her sunglasses. 'Wow that woman is gorgeous,' she thought to herself, her bikini showing off the tan she was starting to get from the warm Spanish sun.

"Hi," Nikki smiled, a little breathless from her manoeuvring between other guests, sunbeds and children's pool toys.

"Hey," Jane returned her smile, gesturing to her left. "I've saved a sunbed for you, and, believe me, it wasn't easy! It nearly started a war!" She laughed.

"Thanks… Have you been down here all morning?" Nikki stretched her towel out on the sunbed and laid down on top of it.

"About two hours. It's beautiful out today. Not a cloud in the sky. Did you sleep well?"

Nikki recalled her dream from the night before and felt herself blush. Busying herself with sun cream, she answered, "Yes, I did, although I think that wine went straight to my head," she giggled. Jane smiled softly. It was nice to see this side of Nikki. Her smiles were few and far between, but today her mood seemed to have lifted. She seemed more relaxed, although there was still that shadow of pain in her eyes that she was trying to hide.

Nikki laid back down after putting on some sun cream. Jane lifted her sunglasses onto her head and looked her up and down.

"That sun tan is coming on well," Jane said,

Turning to face her, Nikki caught that look again. The one she couldn't quite figure out but that, once again, made butterflies dance in her tummy

"You've had a head start! I have some catching up to do." Nikki stretched her arms above her head and sighed contently.

Jane replaced her sunglasses but let her gaze linger a while longer on Nikki's body, taking in the long, toned legs, the little bit of material that covered her womanhood, and the flat stomach leading to her bikini top, showing her cleavage but leaving the rest to the imagination. Feeling the urge to gently run her finger tips down the length of her, Jane quickly turned her gaze away, and lay silently listening to the splashing of the water and the soft murmuring of the guests around the pool.

Both lay appreciating the warmth of the sun in not an uncomfortable silence, but a peaceful silence. Nikki needed this break, but she knew that she would soon have to head back to England and face the inevitable. Even the thought of it made her anxious.

 Michael was constantly calling her, asking her when she was coming home, telling her that they could sort this out, and that things would be OK once they spoke... But she knew that wasn't the case. Without trust, there was no relationship. Their marriage was over, and she had to let Michael know. She had to put the thought of a reconciliation completely out of his head. She had to move on. Plus, there was her father. She loved him dearly, and he was getting on in age and was gradually handing more responsibility over to her in readiness for his retirement. He had built the company from nothing, investing in and selling property all over the world. She loved her work and she felt guilty about leaving her father alone, but he had said time and time again for her to take as much time as she needed. She knew she would have to return soon and tell her father why she had taken off so suddenly – a conversation she didn't relish. Her father had been so happy and proud on the day of her wedding, even shedding a tear as he handed her over to Michael, with the words 'take care of my girl'. He would be devastated at the fact that his one and only daughter's marriage was over. There had been just the two of them for seven years after her mum's death from cancer. He had loved his wife unconditionally and told her so every day of their life together. He wanted the same happiness for Nikki as they had had. She knew it would break his heart when he heard what had happened.

Jane glanced over to where Nikki lay and noticed the smile had faded and a look of sadness had taken over her beautiful face. Wanting to erase that sadness, she broke into Nikki's thoughts.

"So, what are your plans for the rest of the day?" She asked.
Nikki was startled, forgetting where she was, and that Jane was there. Regaining her composure, she turned her head to look at Jane.

"Nothing. I have nothing planned at all. Sorry – I was drifting there".

Jane didn't let on that she had felt the change in her mood. She continued, "How about grabbing something for lunch? I'm going to go for a quick dip and then will go and get showered. I am starting to get hungry."

Nikki realised she, too, was peckish. "That would be lovely," she replied. "I think I've had enough sun for one morning," she laughed. "I will go and get ready while you have your swim and we can meet in the foyer, say – in an hour?"

"It's a date," Jane replied.

Nikki stood up and gathered her belongings. "It's a date," she repeated. "See you soon."

"You will," Jane replied, making her way to the pool edge. She dived into the cool water.

Nikki smiled that dazzling smile and headed towards the hotel. The sight of Jane's firm body dripping with water was doing things to Nikki and she had to drag her gaze away. 'This sun is really going to my head,' she thought to herself as she weaved her way through the now crowded pool area to her room.

Once back in her apartment, Nikki took a quick shower. Hearing her phone ringing, she quickly wrapped herself in a towel and went to answer it.

"Nikki," Michael said. "Nikki, I think you've had enough time to think things over. I'm missing you, baby. I need you to come home. We need to talk – you need to allow me to make this up to you." Remaining silent for a few seconds to gather her thoughts, Michael continued, "Nikki, are you there?"

"I'm here and, yes, we need to sort things out. I will book a flight for the day after tomorrow." "Oh, honey, I knew you would see things differently given time!" Replied Michael. "I have come to my senses Nikki responded, I will check what time the flights are and then let you know what time I will be at the house. I have to call in on dad first, but I will ring you."

The call was ended with Michael relaying how happy he was and how much he had missed her. Nikki hung up, knowing that in a few days' time, he would be feeling very differently. Time away had given her the space she needed to clear her head. This time next week, she would be filing for divorce on the grounds of adultery.

Jane had showered and changed into shorts and a tight t-shirt, her mind full of thoughts of Nikki. All thoughts of her 'no more holiday romances' policy was pushed firmly to the back of her mind, and pretty much forgotten entirely. She liked this woman. There was something about her that seemed to touch her soul. She felt feelings that she didn't think she would know again, and they had started to flow through her. She wanted her so much that she felt the throb of desire between her legs every time Nikki's face entered her mind – but there was something more. Something she didn't want to explore right now. She had promised herself, after Sally, never to commit again. Spraying a light perfume on her neck and wrists, she was ready, and she made her way to the foyer to meet her lunch date.

Nikki was already there, engaged in conversation with the receptionist. Jane hesitated and took a few seconds to run her eyes over Nikki's beautiful figure. Nikki looked lovely in a short, cotton skirt and off-the-shoulder top, her hair falling gently just past her shoulders.
Feeling that now very familiar throb of desire, Jane physically shook herself.

"Sorry I'm late," Jane said, standing close behind Nikki. Jane was near enough to smell the fragrance of Nikki's shampoo, and she had to forcibly stop herself from burying her face in those auburn locks.

Nikki finished her conversation and smiled warmly at Jane, thinking how fit her body looked – not an ounce of fat anywhere. Aglow with health. Fleetingly, their eyes met, but long enough for Nikki to see the hunger in Jane's eyes. For some reason, this gave Nikki a warm feeling, but before she could question herself, Jane said, "Ready?" And, together, they walked out of the hotel into the blazing sun.

It wasn't far to the beach, and the walk was made much quicker by Nikki and Jane's casual chatter about nothing specific. Once at the restaurant, the staff welcomed Jane, obviously knowing her well, and welcomed Nikki on her first visit there.

Seating them both in a quiet corner overlooking the beach, the pretty Spanish waitress gave them a menu each, and left them to make their choice. The soft breeze from the sea was a welcome release from the scorching heat, the soft sounds of the waves hitting the shore was so tranquil.

"It's lovely here," Nikki said. "What a beautiful view! If the food is as good as the surroundings, I'll feel like I've died and gone to heaven," she laughed.

"Believe me, the food is delicious," Jane replied. "Have you decided what you want?"

"Oh – they have Pulpo a la Gallega… I love octopus! I think I'll have that," Nikki said.

"Good choice. I'll have the same. We seem to have the same taste in food," Jane smiled.

Nikki smiled back, only, this time, the smile almost reached her eyes. Jane thought how wonderful it was to see that happen. Nikki's whole face lit up with that smile. She was beautiful and what made her even more appealing was that she didn't seem to know it. How Jane would love to feel those lips on hers... Feeling the desire pulsing through her veins, Jane thought it safer to distract her thoughts by finding out a little more about Nikki.

"What shall we drink?" Jane asked, the remnants of her thoughts still showing in her eyes.

Nikki could see the hunger in them just before Jane looked down at the menu.

"I think just an iced tea for me," Nikki's voice slightly husky, as Jane's look did something to her body.

Jane looked up. "You ok?" She asked, looking at her with concern.

Nikki coughed a little, "I think I have a sore throat coming on," she lied.

"Then iced tea will certainly help ease it," Jane replied.

Jane ordered their meals in perfect Spanish along with one iced tea and one glass of red wine.

"You speak Spanish so well. Was it hard to learn?" Nikki asked, trying for normality while her mind and body felt anything but normal around this woman.

"I took a class, and living here has helped" Jane smiled. "So, Nikki, what about you? What do you do back in England?" Nikki explained that she helped in her father's company, not revealing that it was in fact a multi-million-pound international corporation. She always felt that talking about money was vulgar.

Their conversation was interrupted for a while as their food was brought to the table.

"This looks wonderful," Nikki smiled at the waitress.

"You just wait until you taste it. The flavours dance on the taste buds…" Jane infused.

After tasting her first mouthful, Nikki leant back in her chair with an exaggerated sigh. "Heaven! I've never tasted better." Jane laughed at the pure delight on Nikki's face. "I'm glad you like it! Here's to good food and good company", Jane said, lifting her glass in appreciation of both.

Nikki giggled. "To good food and good company," she repeated as they gently touched glasses.

Their eyes met and, holding each other's gaze, the atmosphere changed – Nikki could feel the sexual charge surrounding them and was the first to look away.

'What the hell was this?' She thought to herself. She had never been sexually attracted to the same sex before yet here she was, her heart beating like a drum against her chest, blushing like a shy teenager. She was sure that Jane was into women. She could tell how confident she was with her sexuality, allowing her desire for Nikki to be seen in her eyes every time she looked at her.

But this was new to Nikki. Was it the emptiness she felt at once again being single? Was it the Spanish sun frazzling her brain? She wasn't sure – nor was she sure she wanted to examine these feelings right now. She had enough going on inside her head without overloading her thought process.

Jane sat and watched the different emotions play across Nikki's face. She didn't want to create a tense atmosphere and push her away, so she went back to small talk, hoping that the easiness they were beginning to feel in each other's company would return.

"So, Nikki, have you decided how long you're staying in Benidorm?" Jane asked.
"I'll be returning to England the day after tomorrow," Nikki replied. "There are so many things that need to be sorted, and that won't happen with me sunning myself in Spain.".
Jane felt like a lead weight had landed in her stomach at the thought of not seeing Nikki again. 'Stupid,' Jane chastised herself. 'You barely know the girl,' thinking now how she should have listened to her own promises not to become involved with women carrying baggage. "So, you're ready to go home?" Jane asked.
"No, but it's something that needs resolving now. My dad is getting on and needs my help at work, so there's no more putting it off. I have responsibilities and a whole lot to sort out.

Like what?" Jane asked, "You don't have to tell me if you don't want to."

Nikki fell silent for a few minutes.

"My divorce," she said softly. "I'm going back to divorce my husband for adultery."

Jane lent forward and placed her hand over Nikki's. "Oh, I'm sorry. For what it's worth, he doesn't deserve you, Nick. Anyone who would cheat on somebody as beautiful as you need their head examined."

Nikki felt the electricity flow through her body at Jane's tender touch but didn't pull her hand away. She also noted that Jane had called her 'Nick' – a shortening of her name that only her father used, but it sounded good coming from the woman sitting in front of her.

"I don't think beauty had anything to do with it," Nikki replied with an edge to her voice. "He thinks with his dick. Honesty is a first in any relationship, along with trust, and without those, there is nothing to work on."

The tears Nikki had thought she had finished shedding now threatened to spill once more.

Sniffing them back, she looked at Jane. "But onwards and upwards as they say."

Jane held Nikki's hand tightly. "When your arse hits the ground, reach for the stars, girl." Nikki smiled that haunted smile that left Jane feeling like she wanted to kiss the pain away.

'Damn that bastard for hurting her,' Jane thought to herself. But that tightening of her tummy at the thought of Nikki leaving stayed with her throughout the rest of the meal, leaving her shuffling her food around the plate – her appetite gone.

They walked back to the apartment in almost complete silence, each lost in their own thoughts.
Once back at the hotel, Jane asked, "Is your flight all booked?"
Nikki nodded her head. "That's what I was speaking to the receptionist about – to make up my bill ready for my departure."
"Then, surely, you can't leave without one last drink?" Jane smiled. "I am double shifting at work tomorrow so this is the last day I have to share your company.
Nikki looked at Jane.
'I'm going to miss this woman,' she thought to herself. A woman she had known for only a few days, but she was going to miss her none the less.
"Sure, why not? I have a bottle of white upstairs, if you don't mind that," Nikki said.
Jane smiled that smile that had Nikki's tummy doing backward flips.
"Then... lead the way," Jane replied, as the lift doors opened.

Once inside the apartment, the space in the lounge seemed to be absorbed by Jane's presence. The energy Nikki felt at the restaurant earlier was magnified. Going to retrieve glasses and pour the wine, Nikki called over her shoulder.
"Feel free to put some music on. There's a CD player over

there in the corner. Not sure if we're into the same music though."

Jane walked over and sorted through the CDs, deciding to put on some Lionel Richie.

"The old ones are the best," Jane said, as the soulful lyrics to 'Hello' filled the room.

"Hmmmm – good choice!" Nikki replied, handing Jane one of the glasses she was holding.

Making her way to one of the sofas, Nikki sat down and sipped her wine, mindful of the effect alcohol had on her. Jane took the seat beside her and, for a while, they sat there listening to the music, each lost in their own thoughts.

"So, what times your flight?" Jane asked.

"8am, so I have booked a taxi, early, for 5:30."

"Are you ready to face those demons you were talking about?"

Nikki turned her head to the side, finding her face just inches from Jane. "No, but it's something I have to do. I can't bury my head in the sand much longer – there are changes that must be made. I must look for a new place to stay. The house will probably go up for sale, so we can split the proceeds."

A sadness took over Nikki's face as she thought about the house she had loved – the work she and Michael had put into it, the beautiful garden that caught the sun in the summer – all tainted and ruined by the events that unfolded that night. Unshed tears shone in her eyes as she recalled all the plans they had – watching their children grow up in the house they had put their hearts and souls into. She felt the pain sear through her being at the realisation that it was truly over. He had taken that happiness she had once felt away. Erased those plans forever. She would never ever forgive him.

Jane saw the pain etched in Nikki's face and automatically reached out and stroked Nikki's cheek.

"Chin up, Nick," Jane said. "I may not know you well, but what I have learnt so far is that you are a very strong, independent woman – you will get there. You'll see."
Nikki didn't move away from Jane's comforting touch. It was soothing and stirred something inside that had her incapable of moving even if she wanted to. Their eyes locked, and Nikki caught her breath as she knew, in that split second, that she was going to experience the kiss of another woman.

Jane leant towards Nikki, placing a kiss gently on her lips, awaiting a response – not wanting to scare her off. When Nikki didn't pull away, she kissed her again, only this time with a little more pressure until Nikki opened her mouth to accept Jane's tongue. Moving closer still, Jane wrapped her hand in Nikki's hair pulling her nearer, closing the distance between them. Nikki's heart was pumping so hard she thought it would break through her chest. Her response was automatic as she deepened the kiss, tongues exploring each other's mouths. Jane gently ran her hand down the front of Nikki's top, softly cupping her breast in her hand. A little gasp escaped Nikki as she felt the warmth of Jane's hand. Nikki put her hands either side of Jane's face, pulling her closer – the moistness between her legs a tell-tale sign of the excitement building inside her. Jane tasted her greedily. This woman had her going crazy. Her body ached for her touch, her own womanhood wet with desire... She wanted Nikki, she needed to feel her naked body under hers. She wanted to explore every bit of exposed skin with her lips. Her kiss deepened further, becoming more urgent. Nikki's body responded with the same increased urgency. The phone rang, breaking the spell they were under, and Nikki pulled away. Looking at the screen, she saw it was Michael and answered the call.

"Yes – I have booked my flight. I'm texting you the details now... No, Michael, I do not want you to meet me at the airport. I told you I'm going to see my dad first, and then coming to the house."

Jane stood up and looked down at Nikki – the hunger still evident in her eyes and the flush of her cheeks.

"Hold on a moment, Michael," Nikki covered the phone with her hand. "I'm sorry – I have to take this call. But, Jane, what just happened? I–" Jane held her hand up to stop Nikki continuing.

"Please don't say it was a mistake," whispered Jane, "Because it wasn't. It was just a moment in time when we both needed someone. Bye Nick – good luck back in England. I will leave you my number. I'll post it under your door in the morning. If you need to talk, I'm just a call away."

Nikki heard the click of the door as Jane left. A hollowness filled her tummy. She would probably never see Jane again, yet the imprint she had left would stay forever. Realising

Michael was still on the other end of the phone, she quickly ended the call, albeit a little more harshly than perhaps she should have.

Making her way out onto the balcony, Nikki felt the early evening sun that was still warm, but she felt a chill around her that had nothing to do with the weather. Sitting on one of the deck chairs, she looked up at the blue sky.

"If only I was in another place at another time," she sighed to herself. But now was not a time for new relationships – even with a person she never imagined herself contemplating a relationship with. She had to focus on settling things back home. She didn't want to enter anything just because she was feeling lonely and sore. That wouldn't be fair to anyone.

****

Michael's head was veering quickly from relief that Nikki was coming home back to the anger he felt for the fact that she had dared to take off without a word. He had decided to play it cool, let her think she was calling all the shots – whatever it took to get her back into his life and, more importantly, into his bed. He was no fool – he knew that, if he lost his marriage, he would also lose his career. The years he had spent climbing the corporate ladder would mean nothing. Old man Roberts would not hesitate to pull that ladder from under him if he didn't get Nikki back, and there was no way he could allow that to happen. She would bare his children and he would take over running the company when her father retired, and she was at home being a mother... So, with this thought in his mind, he set about tidying the house, and making it just right for when she came home.

****

The next day seemed to drag. Nikki hadn't seen Jane at all. She went for breakfast and lunch on her own. She missed Jane and had done nothing but think about the kiss they had shared, her body reacting to the images in her mind. She wanted to see her again before she left for England but remembered she had said she was doing a double shift today. Paying her bill for lunch, Nikki returned to the apartment and packed her stuff – even the beautiful weather couldn't seem to lift her spirits. Then she remembered the telephone number pushed under her door this morning. She dialled the number. She just needed to hear her voice one last time.

Jane didn't feel her normal self today. She usually loved being chatty and friendly with customers, but she didn't feel like engaging in conversation this morning. She was glad the bar where she was working was busy. It prevented her from thinking about Nikki. She knew the kiss they had shared was the first time Nick had kissed a woman, and she didn't want her to think that she was being too full on. Nikki had enough stress waiting for her in England, and, not wanting to be the one to add further pressure, Jane resisted the temptation of leaving work early, so she could go to see her. She walked around the whole day on automatic pilot, her thoughts full of that kiss and what may have happened if Nikki's phone hadn't rung. Images of Nikki's naked body beneath the sheets played round and round in Jane's mind. She could picture her hands on the most intimate parts of Nikki's body, and Nikki calling out her name as she dug her nails into her back as she tasted her. Jane imagined bringing Nikki to the top of the mountain before she fell... spiralling out of control... thrusting her body against Jane's face, forcing her tongue deeper into her as she finally let go, leaving Jane to drink the sweet nectar she had released. A customer's request for the bill brought Jane back down to reality, the dampness between her legs the only evidence of where her mind had travelled.

Jane hadn't answered her phone. All Nikki heard was a pre-recorded message asking her to leave her name and number. "Jane – err – hi. It's Nikki. I–I just wanted to say thank you. Thank you for... Well, everything. I've missed you today, and – err – wanted to give you my number. Give me a call when I'm in England. I would like to know how you are. Bye, Jane, take care."

Nikki hung up the phone with a sigh. This was all so new to her. She didn't know what she should be saying or what she should be doing. She didn't even know if these feelings were real, or just a reaction against what had happened back in England. All she did know was that she missed Jane's company, her smile and the way she looked at her when she said her name. Things were sure going to be different when she got home. Having Jane around made her feel stronger somehow, but now she didn't feel as confident about what she had to face back home alone.

Nikki had spent the whole day and evening alone and was all packed waiting for the taxi to take her to the airport. She scanned the people coming and going from the hotel in the hope that she would see that one familiar face – hoping to see Jane one last time before returning home. "Your taxi is outside, madam," the receptionist called over the foyer. With a heavy heart, and one quick look around, Nikki sighed, and got into the taxi waiting for her.

Jane was rushing through the packed streets of Benidorm, weaving her way through the clubbers. Each one of them seemed to be sent out to prevent her from getting back to The Gemelos in time to see Nick.

Pushing through with an irritated "Excuse me," Jane finally made it to the hotel, hoping she had got back in time to see Nikki. Out of breath and sweating from her fight through the crowds, she approached the old guy on reception.
"Alejandro! Has Miss – err –Miss…" Oh, God, she didn't even know Nikki's last name! "Nikki – you know, the English lady, leaving today – has she gone?" Jane asked in perfect Spanish.
Alejandro looked a little confused, "Which English lady?"
"Nikki. Tall, slim woman. Long auburn hair. Pretty," Jane described, having etched every detail of Nikki onto her memory.
"Oh! Miss Nikki, si. You just missed her. Two minutes. The taxi took her to the airport. Such a beautiful lady, she gave me a big tip, very generous," he smiled.

Jane felt her heart hit the floor. Resting her back against the counter, she surveyed her surroundings. The contentment she had once felt being here was now diminished. She was never going to see that beautiful smile again and would never get another chance to taste those sweet lips. She had come to the realisation that this was more than infatuation over a pretty body and face. Her feelings for Nick went much deeper than that, and to think that she had lost the chance to tell Nikki how she felt just about broke her heart in two.

Entering her apartment, Jane poured a cold drink and sat on the balcony looking at the aeroplanes passing in the sky, wondering if Nick was thinking about her, too. She picked up her phone, feeling lonely and wanting to speak to a friendly voice... And her phone was flashing! She had a missed call! Going into her voicemail, her frown slowly turned into a smile. A warmth filled her body as she heard Nikki's voice. She had her phone number – the moment wasn't lost – she could still tell Nick how she felt!
'I will call her in the morning,' she thought to herself.

Chapter 4: Facing Demons

The aeroplane touched down with a jolt, the harsh rain preventing any view from the window. The weather as miserable as Nikki felt.

She checked into a local hotel where she spent the rest of the day and that night, not quite ready to face Michael or even her father right now. Entering the room, she threw her case on the bed and laid down, fully clothed, on top of the covers. Her mind was back in Spain, and… Jane. She missed Jane. She had got so used to that welcoming smile, the easy way in which she socialised with everyone, and that long, tanned body, stretched out on the sunbed. Nikki felt that tingle between her legs again and shook herself out of her daydream. She needed every ounce of strength to get through tomorrow – a day, she knew, that had to come, but one that she wasn't looking forward to. The only positive was getting to see the gentle face of her father. Sighing, she got to her feet, and ordered room service. After eating very little and watching the rubbish on the television, she had a hot bath and got into bed. But sleep wouldn't come. By the time her eyes closed, the sun had already started to rise.

The portable alarm clock sounded loud in the quietness of the room. Throwing back the covers and rubbing her tired eyes, Nikki walked to the window and looked outside. It was raining, and the clouds were dark, mimicking the way she felt inside. Gone was the cooling invitation of the pool, the hot sun and the sound of laughter. In place of the lines of sunbeds were lines of parked cars, the traffic already heavy, and it was only 7:30am. Taking one last look at the bleakness outside the window, Nikki wrapped her arms around herself and made her way to the bathroom. Looking in the small bathroom mirror, she saw a look of anxiety etched on her face. She got ready to face the end of a chapter in her life.

****

Jane awoke with her knickers damp. She had dreamt of Nikki. Her hands-on Nikki's body, her lips following their pathway, until she found that secret place between her legs. Nick shouting her name as she clawed Jane's back, her fingers working their magic as they entered her slowly and created their own rhythm... Nikki's wetness soaking her hand, her body shuddering as Jane found that precious little bud and circled it with her tongue, flicking and sucking until she felt the crescendo build in her own body, matching Nick's to perfection. Nick's groans of pleasure increasing until she finally found her release once more, and Jane drank from her greedily.

Jane never thought she could miss someone the way she missed her, and the ache she felt in her tummy just thinking of Nick now brought tears to her eyes.

"I'm a stupid woman," she said to herself as she brushed the tears away. "Nothing happened, and nothing will happen. It was just a kiss. Just a holiday crush," she chided herself as she got out of bed and made her way to the bathroom. But somewhere deep down, Jane knew she was lying to herself. She knew that what she felt about this woman was more than a crush, but she was too scared to examine her feelings further so, instead, set the shower too cold to cool off her hot body, and she thought she had succeeded until she listened to her voicemail and heard Nick's voice. Her body flooded again just at the sound of her. Jane smiled at the thought of

Nikki contacting her, and wanting to see her, and wanting Jane to call her back. Heading down to breakfast, Jane went over and over in her head what she would say when she made that call.

****

Deciding to get the worse part of the day over first, Nikki decided to face Michael before seeing her father. Looking at what was once her home brought forth no emotion. She thought that coming back after her time away she would feel something. Maybe sadness at what might have been, or even anger for what happened. But there was nothing. It was as if this was her first time driving up to the front door, as if she were visiting a client, and not about to see her husband. Husband. Even the thought of that word left a sour taste in her mouth. Once upon a time, that was all she ever wanted – to be Michael's wife, to bare his children and be there with baby in arms as he returned from work. But now? Now all she wanted was to erase any memory of him, to tidy up the mess of what was once their marriage and move on. She also knew, from Michael's calls, that he wanted something completely different. He was sure they could fix things. Put things behind them and start again. Well, now was her chance to once and for all put any thoughts like that out of his head and tell him she was filing for divorce.

Using her door keys for what she knew would be the last time, Nikki let herself into the house. She had texted Michael to let him know she was on her way, and his enthusiasm reinforced the fact that she had to put him straight. There was no second chance. No way back. Their marriage was over.

She barely got through the door before Michael was in front of her, pulling her into his arms and holding her so tight as if it by letting her go she would disappear. Nikki allowed the hug to continue for a few moments before shrugging herself out of his arms.

"Hello, Michael."

"Hello, darling. Welcome home," he replied, with that boyish grin on his face.

'Home,' she thought to herself, 'This will never be my home again. Michael needs to understand that.'

"Let's go into the kitchen and talk," Nikki said.

"Sure thing, honey. You must be tired. Let me make you a coffee. Take off your coat and shoes, and I'll put the kettle on." He planted a hard kiss on Nikki's lips and made his way towards the kitchen.

Nikki wiped the back of her hand across her mouth. The feel of his lips on hers was alien to her now. Gone was the giddiness she felt every time he touched her. Her thoughts went back to somebody else's lips on hers – soft gentle lips – lips that left her feeling weak and wanting more. She felt the wetness between her legs at the thought of Jane.

"Nikki, coffee is ready, darling," Michael's voice jolted her back to the present.

With a blush still lingering on her cheeks, Nikki took her coat off and, leaving her shoes on, walked towards the kitchen.

****

Jane had finished her morning shift at the Union Jack and was sat at one of the tables with an iced tea. She had her phone in her hands. For the past 10 minutes, she had sat staring at the screen, going over in her head what she would say to Nick when she heard her voice. Not feeling quite brave enough to call, she decided on a text first. Maybe Nikki had forgotten her already – something she didn't want to hear in her voice, so a text seemed to be the safest option. Tapping in a message, Jane pushed 'send' before the temptation of deleting it took over. Leaning back in her chair, she took a deep breath, and wondered – prayed even – that Nick would reply. Her days didn't feel so bright anymore, and her nights were even longer without Nick here. Thoughts of returning to England to visit her family had been running through her head, knowing that the real reason for wanting to return was in the hope that she would see Nick again – that they could meet for a coffee and that Jane could tell her that she hadn't stopped thinking about her and that she would say the same.

****

Nikki had just sat down at the kitchen table when she heard the bleep of her phone. Taking it from her handbag, she felt her stomach somersault as she saw it was a text from Jane. Opening the message quickly, she read its contents.

'Hi Nick, hope you're OK. Was just sitting here thinking of you. Thinking you need to come back and finish off that sun tan! Miss you, hope everything is going OK, give me a call when you get a minute, if you want to, of course. Would be nice to hear your voice again. Love Jane x'

Nikki smiled as she returned the message.

'Hi Jane, I'm fine, hope you are too. Maybe after I've finished what needs taking care of here, I can think about working on my tan. If it's ok with you, I will give you a call around 6pm my time, would be good to hear your voice too. Love Nikki x'

"Who's making you smile?" She heard Michael ask. Nikki looked up to see a petulant look on his face.

"Not that I should have to explain, but it was a friend I met when I was away. Jane. She was very sweet to me."

She instantly saw Michael's features soften as he heard it was a woman, "I'm glad you found a friend, darling. After what I put you through, I can imagine you needed someone to talk to."

Nikki sipped her coffee and came out with it.

"Michael, I'm filing for divorce."

Michael felt the blood drain from his face. "A divorce? But, Nikki, I thought I explained how sorry I was. We can fix this, darling. You're just angry. I know it will take time to put things right – for you to trust me again – but we can do this. We love each other."

"Please, Michael, stop it." Nikki replied. "What you did I can never forgive you for. In our house, in our bedroom, in that one instant you took everything we had planned and destroyed it. We can't go back. Well, at least, I can't. I'm sorry, Michael. I know it's not what you wanted to hear. But our marriage is over."

Nikki slumped back in her chair. It seemed to squeeze every ounce of energy finally saying what had been going around in her head since that night.

"Michael, I—"

"No, Nikki." Michael stopped her mid-sentence. "No, I can't let this happen. You can't leave me! We are meant to be. You're just letting your emotions take over. In time, you will forget about this and—

"My emotions!" Nikki interrupted. "Of course, my emotions are involved! You hurt me, Michael. You cheated on me with my best friend in our bedroom."

Shaking her head at this man's pig-headedness, she continued.

"You really do take the piss, Michael. You can't let this happen? It's because of you this is happening!" Rising to her feet, Nikki continued. "Some things can't be fixed, Michael. This is one of those things. I am going to see a solicitor tomorrow. I need to move on. I will call you tomorrow and maybe we can arrange things civilly without the need for lawyers."

Nikki took one last look at her husband, then walked past where he sat, and headed towards the door. Suddenly, she felt him grip her arm and swing her around.

"You can't do this to me," he growled. "I said I'm sorry. What else do you want?" His face was flushed red with anger, just a few inches from her own.

"Michael, let go of me. You're hurting me."

"You're not divorcing me Nikki. You love me," he crushed his lips against hers forcing his tongue into her mouth, but the more she struggled, the harder he gripped her, until, in the end, he let out a yelp. Nikki had bit his tongue. He let her go immediately.

"You bit me," he said looking at her as if he couldn't believe she hadn't succumbed to his kiss.

Nikki grabbed her coat and opened the front door. "That is the last time you ever touch me," she hissed through gritted teeth. "If you ever touch me like that again, I will add assault to the charge of adultery."

She slammed the door hard behind her.

Michael stared at the door, wondering who this new, determined woman was. If she divorced him, he would lose everything. She loved him once and she would love him again. He walked back towards the kitchen and the bottle of whisky in the cupboard.

Nikki parked in her reserved parking space outside her father's home. She wiped the back of her hand across her lips, trying to erase the imprint of Michael's kiss. She felt the bruising left the by his onslaught. Her arm was sore where he had grabbed her, and she feared there would be marks left by his rough handling. She had never known him to be aggressive before. He had always been so gentle with her.

Taking a deep breath, she put her key into the familiar lock of her family home, bracing herself for the conversation she was going to have with her dad. Her father, having heard her key turn in the door, was in the hallway ready to greet her. Grabbing her into a bear hug, she snuggled safely into his shoulder and the flood gates opened. He held her while she cried, whispering soothing words into her hair, holding her tightly until the tears subsided and all that was left were the little sobs she couldn't control.

Holding her at arm's length, he looked at his daughter. She looked thinner and, although she had caught the sun, he could still see the pallor beneath her skin. He knew she was hurting but didn't push. Instead, he leads her into the lounge. The huge windows were still curtained in the same material her mother had once chosen. She kicked off her shoes and felt the comfort of the thick piled carpet beneath her feet as her father guided her to one of the other stuffed chairs, sat her down and placed a brandy in her hand.

Nikki looked around the room. Memories of family dinners and parties flooded through her mind, her mother in her element as she hosted these events, a soft look in her eyes as she looked at her husband. The pale green walls made the room peaceful and welcoming, despite its size. The baby grand her mother had taught her to play still stood proudly in the corner of the room covered in silver-framed photographs of different periods in her life, from baby to the adult she was now. How she missed her mother, and, looking across the room at the look of concern on her father's face, she knew he missed her too. If ever there was love, they shared it.

Her father waited patiently for Nikki to talk, knowing she was feeling the same emotions he felt every time he walked into this room – memories of laughter and love and the longing for what had been and was now gone. How he wished he could wipe the sadness from his daughter's face. He felt the blood boil in his veins at whoever put it there.

Eventually, after a few sips of the brandy, Nikki started to speak.
"Dad, I'm divorcing Michael."
Her father sat silently, knowing there had been tension between them, but not realising that things had got this bad. Still, he remained quiet, allowing his daughter to explain what had been going on and why she looked so desolate.

Nikki relayed the whole story from beginning to end, only leaving out the part about Jane. Even she was still examining her feelings about the woman she left in Spain
"...And that's what happened. I can't stay married to someone who I have no trust or faith in anymore. I'm so sorry, I know how happy you were when we told you about our marriage, and how you welcomed Michael into the family with open arms..."

Her father silenced her.

"Your happiness is my only concern, Nikki. To think that... that... animal... that son of a bitch could hurt you so badly..."

She saw the tears in her father's eyes. The clenching of his fists as he tried to contain his anger. She went over to him. Kneeling on the floor in front of the man she loved dearly, she rested her head in his lap.

"Please, daddy, please don't cry. I'm fine, honestly, I am. I just want to move on and put this part of my life behind me. I want to find someone to love and who will love me back in the way you and mummy did."

Her mind recalled Jane's face as she spoke these words. She remembered her soft lips on hers and the bikini-clad body stretched out on a sun lounger. God, she missed her.

"My darling child," her father's voice cut into her thoughts. "I am here. I will always be here for you and whatever you need, whatever support I can give you, I will provide. I love you, Nikki, and I want you to be happy. I want to see that fabulous smile that so looks like your mothers replace the sadness on your face. You can't go back there, Nikki. You can stay here in your old room until things are settled. You don't have to go through this alone. You are never alone."

The gentleness in her father's voice had her crying once more, and she laid there on his lap with him stroking her hair for what seemed like hours.

"Come now, Nikki. You look exhausted. Have you eaten? Shall I get Maria to make you something?"

Nikki shook her head, "I'm not hungry, but I am tired." Raising to her feet, she kissed her dad softly on the cheek. "Tomorrow is another day," she smiled gently at him. "I love you, dad."

Kissing the back of her hand, he wished her goodnight and smiled lovingly at his daughter as she left the room.

'If that man, that fool, Michael, still thought he had a place in this family – in the family business – then he was sadly mistaken. He held the position he did because he was married to my daughter,' Nikki's father thought. 'Because he had promised to love and cherish her. But first thing tomorrow, Michael will be fired, and I will get great pleasure in seeing him crumble. I made him, and now I'll break him.' Nikki's father had his fists clenched on his lap, recalling the pain in his daughter's eyes.

Nikki was laying on her bed. Nothing had changed in her old bedroom. She felt at ease here, snuggled in the comfort of her memories. It had been a long day; her head was foggy and her eyes heavy. She felt them closing and thought she was dreaming when she heard her mobile ring. Warily eyeing the name on the phone, believing it to be Michael begging her to change mind, she was a little confused when the word 'international' flashed up on the screen.

Placing the phone to her ear, she sleepily said, "Hello? Nikki speaking."

"Hi Nick. It's me, Jane. I wanted to make sure you got home safely and wanted to check on how you are doing. I know you had some hard conversations today." Nikki felt instantly better and reassured at the sound of Jane's voice.

"Jane," Nikki's voice was warm and welcoming, "I was thinking about you. I'm sorry I didn't ring at 6 but it's been an awful day."
"I bet it has, Nick. I wanted to make sure you were OK. And, well, I was missing your voice. How did it go today?"

Nikki felt the now familiar butterflies and warmth in her groin, knowing that Jane was missing her voice, and replied, "I have missed the sound of your voice, too, Jane – and believe me, you don't want to know how it went. But the main thing is that I have told Michael I want a divorce and explained all to my father, who was a tower of strength.

Jane smiled softly to herself, glad that she wasn't a distant memory and that Nikki missed her too. "I can't imagine how hard today must have been for you. I wanted to call and make sure you were OK."

"I'm OK. Thank you. Just drained," Nikki replied. "I don't know how I would have got through today without the support of my father. He has been amazing."
"And you, Jane, how are you? I miss our lazy mornings sunbathing, especially since it's done nothing but rain since I got back."", Nikki sighed

"Well, there's plenty of sun here if you feel like returning," Jane said, her whole body and mind crying out for Nickki, but keeping her voice light and playful, "Just let me know when and I will reserve the room," she laughed.

"Oh, don't tempt me," Nikki laughed back. "But I think my poor, old father would have a fit if I upped and left again so soon. As soon as I have ironed things out here, I'm sure I'll deserve another well-earned rest, so hold that thought."

Promising to stay in touch, their call ended. They both missed the sound of each other's voices instantly.

This following morning was grey and dismal – not unusual for England – but seemed to match Nikki's mood. Knowing she would have to go into the office and face Michael (and a barrage of questions asking where she'd been and why she left so quickly), she wasn't feeling enthusiastic about it. Grimacing at her reflection in the mirror, she decided extra makeup was needed today to cover the worry lines she saw so clearly around her eyes.

Chapter 5: You're Fired

Dressed in a navy blue trouser suit and with briefcase in hand, Nikki looked the suave, confident business woman that belied her inner emotions. Hailing a taxi, she took the back seat and gave the driver the address to her office. Sitting quietly, contemplating the day ahead, she noticed she had started to bite her nails – a habit she had given up as a child when her mother told her she would end up eating her fingers, too, if she wasn't careful. The memory of her mother brought a smile to her lips – the things her mother had told her to discourage her from bad habits and that she had taken as gospel you wouldn't believe.

Still feeling anxious about her first day back and the obvious awkward questions about why she had been away, she asked the driver to drop her off a few streets from the office, so she could walk off some of the tension and be better prepared to face the day.

Her father, a formidable business man, had got to his company early, dressed in a grey pinstriped suit and his short grey hair neatly groomed. He was the exact image everyone had of a high flyer, confidence oozing from every pore and a presence that demanded respect.

Everyone greeted him with a, "Good morning, Mr Roberts," as he passed through the various employees. Nodding his head in acknowledgement, he took large purposeful strides towards his office where his PA was already at her desk.

"Good morning, Mr Roberts. There are messages on your desk waiting for you. Can I get you a coffee?"
"Morning, Brenda," he smiled. He liked Brenda. She was always well-groomed, and was the sole of discretion, which was important in a business such as his. He relied on her heavily but paid her a good salary with bonuses in return.

"Brenda, as soon as Michael, arrives would you tell him I want to see him immediately? And hold all my calls until I say, and, yes, a coffee would be lovely. Thank you."

Brenda, having worked for this man for many years, could sense the purpose in him today – a suppressed anger simmering just below the service. Having seen him in action with those who had crossed him in the pass, she felt sympathy for whoever was in the line of fire today.

"Of course, Mr Roberts. I will send him into your office as soon as he arrives," Brenda replied, leaving her desk to get the coffee she had offered.

Michael pulled up in the reserved parking. Straightening his tie and sucking a mint in the hope he would disguise the heavy night of drinking he had indulged in, he entered the building. He knew Nikki wasn't at work yet. Her car wasn't in the space reserved next to his. He was glad he had arrived before her. He wanted to gauge her mood before asking her out to dinner to discuss things once more. A little wine, some gentle coaxing and some gentle love-making should help her change her mind about the divorce, make her realise she still wanted him and that she needed him in her life.

Michael made his way through the offices, feeling pleased that Nikki had already dismissed Ashley. It would have been too awkward to share the same workplace with the person whom he'd had a fling with.

As he passed by Brenda, he gave a little nod and went to walk by to get to his office, but Brenda called after him.

"Mr Roberts would like to see you straight away, Michael."

"OK, Brenda. I have a few calls to make first and then I'll be right there," he replied.

"Mr Roberts said immediately. He doesn't seem very happy. I wouldn't recommend you make him wait."

The hairs on the back of the Michael's head stood up. 'Surely he didn't know anything. No, of course not,' he thought to himself. 'Nikki wouldn't have told her father any of this. She wouldn't have been able to bring herself to do so.'

But still that uneasy feeling persisted. He knocked on the door.

"Come in."

Michael opened the door and walked towards John's desk. "Hi, John. I heard you wanted to see me – is there a problem?"

John looked up from the paperwork he was trying to read. "Not for long, Michael," he replied, gesturing for Michael to take a seat in the chair opposite him.

Michael smoothed his hand down his tie, bringing attention to his half-ironed shirt.

"Well, whatever I can do to help, just say. After all, that's what I'm here for."

Still feeling uneasy, Michael began to fidget with his wedding ring – something he often did when he was feeling unconfident or worried about something.

John took in Michael's look of discomfort and took great pleasure in it.
"Is your wedding ring irritating you?" he asked, looking directly into Michael's eyes. "Or maybe it's burning you a little?"

"I don't understand what you mean. It's become a little lose, that's all. I've been meaning to get it adjusted but– "
"Things like that happen Michael," John interrupted.
"Especially to filthy, low-life, cheating scumbags."
"Filthy, low-life scum? Do you want to explain what this is all about John?" Michael asked, already knowing in the pit of his stomach that the old man knew about his infidelity.

"Now that little problem I was talking about... Let's get it sorted, shall we?" John started, making his way around the desk. Placing a hand either side of Michael's chair, their noses almost touching, John's voice came out at barely a whisper, but the menace under his words was clearly audible.
"Get yourself out of this office, out of this building and out of my daughter's life, before my coffee goes cold or I will get you thrown out like the vermin you are."

Michael pushed himself out of the chair, matching John's height but not matching John's confidence. In a voice he hoped sounded formidable but, in truth, belied the trepidation he felt, Michael replied.

"Don't tell me what to do regarding my marriage John. It's between me and Nikki. I'm sorry this happened – it's all my fault but you can't dictate to either of us about what happens in our lives."

John's laugh was low. "Michael, you have no life. You leave this marriage as you entered it – with nothing. You break my girl's heart, I destroy you. That's all there is to it. Now my coffee is almost cold, so get yourself out of this building before I bust your nose all over that face of yours. Oh, and tell Ashley good luck in finding another job, too. It will be just as impossible in this town as it will be for you."

"John, listen, please," Michael stuttered. "It didn't mean anything. I promise you– "

John swung back around to face his daughter's betrayer.

"Well it did to Nikki. Now you are on your last warning. Get the fuck out."

Opening the door, John pushed Michael through it and slammed it shut.

Everyone stopped what they were doing and turned to look at the commotion. The office fell silent as Michael stomped through the hallway towards his office, his eyes meeting theirs as they quickly looked away in the pretence of getting on with their work.

Slamming his door behind him, Michael yanked off his tie and threw his briefcase across the room. "Bitch!" he said aloud to himself. That bitch had told the one person she knew would destroy him. He needed a drink. Going to his desk, he retrieved a bottle of brandy from the drawer that was usually kept for clients. Unscrewing the lid, he took a swig directly from the bottle.

Michael picked up a silver-framed photo of their wedding day. They both looked so happy – all their dreams just beginning. And then he smiled. Not a soft, sad smile, but an 'I will get you back' smile. Nikki was his wife. He would do whatever it took to get her back into his life and his bed. He would get her pregnant, and if that old goat ever wanted to see his grandchild, he would have to get down on his knees and beg. The only thing that would ever give that old bastard any chance of seeing his princess or their child would be 51 percent of the company, or it would be goodbye forever, and he knew John could never let that happen. Retrieving his briefcase and placing both the frame and bottle of brandy inside, he left the building, feeling a little bit better. Although he knew taking on John Roberts was not going to be easy.

Getting into his car, he sat for a while. He felt nauseous and needed to calm down before driving away. And then he caught sight of her.

Looking every inch, the business woman with an air of confidence, Nikki walked into the building. She looked beautiful, Michael thought, and the movement in his trousers confirmed the effect she had on him. He knew that he would have great pleasure in taking this woman to his bed and impregnating her. With that thought and a smile on his lips, he reversed out of the parking space and headed towards home.

Chapter 6: Yearning

The happiness that Benidorm used to bring Jane had seemed to have diminished since Nik left. The blues skies, white sand – even the sun shining – couldn't lift her spirits. In just a few short days, that woman had got under her skin. She sat on the balcony remembering that kiss, imagining what could have happened if that phone hadn't rung. Jane thought about running her tongue down Nikki's naked torso. It had her damp with desire. She could almost hear her groans as she gently slipped inside her, Nikki's juices running down her hand as she fucked her.

"My God!" Jane said aloud. If she didn't stop this now, she would orgasm from the scenario playing through her mind. She had to see Nikki again. She needed to know if this was something more than a holiday fantasy. She needed to know if Nikki could feel the same pulsing needs that she felt. Sighing heavily and with darkness falling, Jane took herself to bed, but these images returned in her dreams, lips on lips, tongues entwined, her face pushed against Nikki's throbbing womanhood… She awoke with her own hand inside her panties, rolling her finger around her swollen bud. Fantasizing that it was Nikk's hand, she brought herself to fulfilment, whispering Nick's name into her pillow as she fell back to sleep.

With morning came the same yearning she couldn't stand any longer. She had to go and find out exactly what 'this' was. Making her decision and smiling to herself as she finished her coffee, Jane set off to tell her bosses that she needed a little holiday back home.

She would call Nikki tonight, hoping that she, too, would be as excited as she felt right now. Feeling better than she had since Nikki left, she sang softly to herself as she made her way to work.

****

Nikki was feeling anxious at the thought of coming face to face with Michael again – especially after their last encounter. Faking a smile and straightening her back, Nikki stepped out of the lift.

Everyone seemed really pleased to see her again, commenting on how well she looked and that her 'holiday' had obviously done her the world of good. Responding with a smile and acknowledgment of their well wishes, she glanced nervously over towards Michael's office. The door was open, but the room was empty. She felt herself release the breath she hadn't realised she'd been holding.

"Hi, Brenda," she greeted her father's secretary, walking past." Is the old man in yet?"

"Nikki, you look wonderful," Brenda responded warmly. "Yes, he was in early today. Go on in – I'm sure he will be pleased to see you."

Knocking on her father's door and not waiting for a response, Nikki entered her father's office. John rose from his desk and went to meet her with that big, warm smile of his.

"Nik, darling, you look wonderful. It's good to have you back."

"It's good to be back, Dad," she replied, placing a kiss on his cheek. "I see Michael's not in yet – gives me time to compose myself. I've been dreading having to see him. I just know the staff will pick up that there's a problem with any kind of atmosphere."

"Oh, he's already been in", her father replied. "You don't every have to worry about bumping into him again. Well, not at the office, anyway, darling. He's gone for good."

Nikki looked at her father, seeming somewhat confused. He continued.

"I fired him first thing and told him in no uncertain terms that he will never work again in this town as long as there's breath in my body."

Nikki looked into her dad's kind eyes and then, placing her hands either side of his face, replied.

"Thank you. It would've been almost impossible to come into work knowing I would have to face him every day. But that's all that was needed – I don't want or need any type of revenge."

Her father opened his mouth to speak but Nikki continued. "I just want to get on with my life. I don't want any animosity or drama. Everything that's happened nearly broke me. I want to get through this divorce with as little heartache as possible. Please, Dad – please promise me you won't get involved."

John looked into his daughter's eyes. She always did have a big heart just like her mother.

"OK," he replied. "On two conditions."

Nikki drew her brows together. "Which are?"

"That I take my beautiful daughter out to dinner and get her the best divorce lawyer in town," her father smiled.

"It's a deal," Nikki replied, kissing her father on the forehead.

Chapter 7: No One Else

After a good day a work and securing the sale of a £1.5 million property in Blackheath, Nikki decided to pop into a quaint little coffee shop that was just a 10-minute walk from her father's house, a flat white would go down just right round about now she thought to herself.

Taking her coffee to a window seat she watched the hustle and bustle of commuters getting of their buses and making their way home, she loved people watching, even as a child she used to sit with her mother and try to guess what type of job or life these people had by the type of work clothes they wore.

Her mind wandered back to Benidorm and Jane, she missed her and the sound of her voice, just the recall of her face had those now familiar butterflies taking flight inside her tummy and her dreams will still filled with soft hands and tender love making. 'I will call her' she thought to herself the prospect of talking to her seemed to attract even more butterflies. Taking out her mobile phone she was just about to search contacts when it started ringing, the name Jane flashed up on the screen. Nikki's heart felt like it had missed a beat as she answered the call with a ''Jane, great minds and all that I was just about to ring you.

"Were you really Nick" Jane responded, a smile plastered all over her face. The sound of her name on Janes lips had Nikki's panties damp and her twisting in her seat.

"Nick, can you hear me?" bringing her back to reality Nikki replied "yes yes I can here you I'm in a coffee shop and its quite noisy in here" she lied, blushing slightly at where her mind had been taking her. "You will have to speak up."

"How have you been Nick, how are things going I've been thinking of what a hard time you must be having right now, "oh I'm getting there slowly but there's a way to go yet." How are you Jane? It's great to hear from you, anything exciting happening in Benidorm?"

On hearing that Nikki had been thinking of her caused Janes heart beat to speed up so coming to the point of the call she replied "I have two weeks holiday owed to me and am planning a visit to my family in England, I thought it would be cool if we could meet up, that's if you're not too busy, I'm hoping to fly out on Saturday."

Almost choking on her coffee Nikki couldn't hide her pleasure at this news, "Oh Jane that would be wonderful, of course I won't be too busy, I could even pick you up from the airport if you like."

That would be great if you could Nick, I will text you the details when everything is booked is that ok?" "Of course, its ok", her own heart doing summersaults "just send me the details and I will be there."

I will, right I must get some beauty sleep I have work early tomorrow and I don't want to be scaring any customers, do I?" Jane laughed. "Oh, you won't need much sleep then" Nikki replied blushing furiously at her attempt at … at what? Flirting? "Why thank you kindly but there's no denying the mirror I'm afraid Jane laughed again, easing the awkwardness she felt flow down the line and liking Nikki even more for it.

After some more small talk and promising to send her flight details added "I've missed you Nick" "and I've missed you Jane they both said their goodbyes and hung up the phone. Jane's heart was singing as she said out loud to her apartment "she misses me, she said she misses me and with that thought on her mind her dreams that night consisted of unruly auburn hair and the softest skin she had every touched.

As Nikki's call ended her phone rang again this time displaying Michael's name. Thinking of not answering it and then chastising herself 'of course there would need to be communication' she thought to herself, so answering the phone "hello" she said.

"Nikki please don't hang up I don't want any more arguments and I'm so sorry for what happened the other day, too much drink and I apologise." "I am more rational now, and Nikki we need to talk, if this is really what you want, "and I can't say I blame you honey", then we need to sort this and sort it as amicably as possible. "This is all my fault and I will agree to whatever your attorney say's so as not to cause you any more pain and make this as easy as possible."

Nikki wasn't sure if she had heard him right, such a big change in the way he had behaved when they had last met up and she said so, "why the change of heart Michael, I would have thought you would be even more angry, especially after what happened between you and my father today."

"As I said," Michael replied, "I have come to my senses, which is easier to do without alcohol in the body, and everything your father said hit home Nikki, I hurt you and for that I could never forgive myself so how could you forgive me." I don't want to hurt you any more Nikki, I want you to have in your life what makes you happy so I'm willing to do my part in that."

"Can we meet, at your convenience of course and discuss what happens next, like the house sale etc, I could come to you or you could come here one evening after work if you prefer," Michael continued.

This Michael reminded Nikki of the Michael she had married, the kind gentle man, not the aggressive fuelled by alcohol type of man he was the other day, she had to concede that although the end of their marriage was of his doing, this would obviously be painful for him to.

"Yes, yes, that would be fine Michael, all I want is for us to do this without any pain or point scoring, thank you Michael you don't know how much stress you have eased, I will check my Diary at the office tomorrow and give you a call as too when I can call in and see you, is that ok?"

"That fine Nikki, thank you for giving me another chance you could have just left it all to the solicitors after the way I behaved, so yes please do Nikki, give me a message letting me know what's good for you and let's get the ball rolling."
"Bye Nikki have a nice evening." And with that Michael hung up the phone.

Nikki looked at her phone wondering if she had imagined the conversation that had just taken place, but happy in knowing that things were going to be a lot easier from now on."

Nikki left the café, she had to get ready for the dinner date with her father, with the prospect of seeing Jane again she felt giddy inside like a child waiting for the morning to bring Christmas.

The next morning she drove too work, the radio on loud and the weather feeling warmer, she hadn't felt this good in a while, she had received Janes flight details and in just a few more days she would be seeing her again, this is what kept the smile on her face as she pulled into her parking space at work and entered the building

Chapter 8: That Knowing look

John Roberts had noticed the sudden change in his daughter, she had been smiling a lot more these last couple of days, even catching her daydreaming and blushing when she realised he had been watching her, he didn't know who had put that smile on her lips, but he would like to shake their hand.

"You are absolutely glowing" John said to Nikki whilst giving Brenda a list of calls to be returned. "Am I" Nikki replied, a rosy tint forming on her cheeks. "You sure are" interjected Brenda, these last few days have had you walking on air, who's the lucky man"? Nikki blushed a deep red, "I can ensure you there is no 'lucky man', trying to keep the smile off her face but failing miserably.

Brenda looked at John and gave him a wink and he winked back. "I really don't know what those looks are for Nikki chastised them both, there is nothing going on in my private life, and if there were I wouldn't take to kindly it being discussed in front of all and sundered," and with a huff and straightening of her shoulders she marched back towards her office. Both John and Brenda watched her go smiling to themselves "she has it bad" Brenda stated, John watched he's daughter until she disappeared into her office, whoever It was had better not hurt her, she'd had had enough hurt in her young life he thought to himself.

Nikki left work a little earlier that day, wanting to do some shopping so as she could cook her father and herself an evening meal, she liked it when it was just the two of them, father and daughter time she thought to herself. Another reason for leaving early is that she wanted to make a call from the privacy of her father's home, she wanted to call the lawyers her father had hired for her, their courier was delivering the divorce petition by hand to Michael today.

Arriving home and putting the shopping on the kitchen counter Nikki lifted the receiver and dialled the number to Barratts and Barratts family lawyers, the receptionist confirmed that the document had been delivered at 4pm that afternoon continuing "the courier said that after snatching the letter from his hand that Mr lever (Michael) had slammed the door so hard he thought it might fly from its hinges, although this isn't unusual in these circumstance" she related. Thanking her for her time, Nikki hung up the phone and began chewing on her bottom lip, she hopped that this hadn't set the cat amongst the pigeons so to speak and had veered Michael off the path of amicability onto that of anger once again. Walking into the kitchen to start preparing dinner she told herself she would ring him later and test the water.

John Roberts opened the door to his family home and was instantly rewarded with the armour coming from the kitchen, he stopped for a little in the hallway, memories flooding back of times he had returned home and found his wife and a 'little Nikki' both wearing aprons with flour all over their faces and giggles about the funny shapes of the cakes they had just baked. Oh, how he still yearned for those days, he could still recall the smell of his wife's perfume as he hugged her close as she had welcomed him home, and the smaller arms of his daughter being wrapped around his legs. Life had seemed to have stopped for him, the moment she had taken her last breath, or it would have done if it wasn't for Nikki. He would have been quite happy to have stayed in bed all day and all night until he faded away into oblivion. "Daddy, Daddy, please get up, I need to ge tthings ready for school tomorrow, mummy use to leave out my uniform and now I don't know where it is," said a tearful Nikki, "do you think she's cross with me is that why she gone away?" "John looked into the tear-filled eyes of his daughter and saw his wife looking back at him, "NO darling, oh no, mummy loved you very much, remember we told you she was poorly and had to go and find the brightest star in the sky, so we can see her every night?" Nikki nodded her head, "can we look out of the window daddy, will she be there?" John lifted her in his arms as they walked towards the window, and there was the brightest star he had ever seen, pointing it out to Nikki "look there she is sweetheart, she's always with us", Nikki followed her father's gaze and looked intently into his face, lips wobbling she asked "you don't need to find a star do you daddy?" "No, my darling, I have my star right here." And from then he knew he had to keep it together, he had to be there for this sad little girl who missed her mummy so very much. Nikki was the reason he got up of a morning, the reason he worked so hard, he wanted her to not need or want for anything when he's time came.

"Dad, your home" John was brought back to the present by the sound of his daughter's voice. "I am indeed, and something smells good," "Are you hungry, dinner is ready we just need the wine from the fridge," Starving her father replied as she took his hand and lead him to the kitchen.

After eating John stretched back in his chair patting his stomach, I couldn't eat another thing, that was wonderful Nick, I see it wasn't just beauty you inherited from your mother" he smiled. "I'm glad you enjoyed it, I like looking after you, it makes a change" Nikki replied. "Oh, by the way I called the lawyer today and they confirmed that the petition of divorce had been served on Michael today, according to the courier he was none too happy."

"Don't let that bother you honey, he's probably realising what he has lost and all of he's own doing. " I know" Nikki replied looking down into her dinner plate as she recalled the images of that afternoon, it all seemed so long ago now, "I had spoken to him earlier and he agreed he wanted this to all be as amicable as possible, I just hope this don't change he's mind." "He knows what's good for him" her father replied, "he's doing you no favours darling, he just doesn't want his name dragged through the mud, it won't look very good on he's next cv," Nikki thought this over, "I suppose your right" she replied feeling a little better now. "Is it ok if a friend stays here Saturday I'm collecting them from the airport on Saturday, someone I met whilst in Benidorm." Her father rose he's eye brows, "a friend you say, and pray may I ask he's name?" "He is a she Nikki giggled at her father's look, and her name is Jane." Her dad smiled at her "a girlfriend, it's just I thought that maybe you had found someone ermmmmm special." Nikki fell silent for a while and then responded, "Maybe I have." Her father looked at her a little confused, "sit down dad I will pour some wine, I want to tell you about everything that happened when I was in Benidorm."

"And so, you see," Nikki continued coming to the end of her story I'm not sure really what's happening, whether this is a rebound thing or if my feelings for Jane go deeper." Her father listened intently to his daughter "are you disappointed in me dad"? Nikki asked dubiously.

John stood up from his chair and walked over to his daughter, holding her hand she stood facing him. "You could never be a disappointment to me Nick, never, your happiness is all I'm interested in, not who you find that happiness with."

Nikki flung herself into her father's arm, "Oh dad, how did I deserve a father as wonderful as you, so strong, supportive and most of all loving." "By being your amazing wonderful self," he replied kissing her forehead, now for another glass of wine, "to loving families her father toasted, "to loving families echoed Nikki.

Nikki awoke early the next morning.
"Today's the day,' she thought to herself.
Jane's flight was due and she was feeling excited and anxious all at the same time. She had eased her fears regarding Michael. She had phoned him and, although admitting that he hadn't accepted the petition with anything other than sadness and anger, he was still prepared to give her what she wanted. So, with her problems seeming far behind her, she ran a hot scented bath. Climbing into the steamy, fragrant water, she let herself relax, and her mind took her back to that day in Benidorm.

That kiss made her feel something she had never felt before. She felt her need heighten as she played out a senario in her head of those warm soft kisses. Slowly, she slid her hand between her legs, searching for the place she knew would bring her release. Finding the hot moistness of her most intimate part, she began stroking herself, imagining her hand was Jane's hand exploring her body. They were soft gentle hands that caressed every part of her, cupping her breasts then replacing her hand with her tongue, letting her tongue guide her down to where she knew she was needed while Nikki whimpered and groaned. Lifting her hips to meet Jane's hungry mouth, she thought she would explode when her tongue found the hardened bud of her womanhood and swirled around it, sending shocks all over her body. Nikki's breathing became more erratic as the rhythm increased, sending her mind swirling in the sky high above her body, sucking and licking the very centre of her soul. Jane brought her closer and closer to the edge. Crescendo after crescendo of building inside her until, finally, she could not contain this feeling any more. With a scream of Jane's name on her lips, she exploded into a million pieces, filling Jane's mouth with the nectar within. Swirling. Swirling until her feet finally landed firmly on solid ground. The intenseness of the orgasm Nikki had experienced whilst touching herself she had never felt before. She slowly lifted herself from the tub, still throbbing, and wrapped herself in towel. She looked in the mirror as she left the bathroom and saw the face of a wanton woman. What was this girl doing to her? Even more intent on exploring the answer to the question, she hurried to get dressed.

The airport was a buzz of activity when Nikki arrived, people either arriving from their destinations or others waiting for their return. Taking a look at the information board, she noticed she still had 20 minutes before Jane's plane landed, so she made her way to the coffee shack nearby. Buying herself a latte, she sat at an empty table, trying to calm her mind by people watching. She noted a man and woman having an animated argument, and trolleys with a mind of their own, filled with luggage zig-zagging around in whichever direction they chose, some even with children perched on top of the cases, looking tired and in need of their beds.

By the time Nikki finished her coffee and she checked the information board again, Jane's luggage was in the hall, and that familiar but intense start of the butterfly dance began in her stomach.

Nearing the arrival barriers holding eager families back, Nikki paced up and down, looking for Jane. She slalomed in and out of the people with placards with names on them, held high in the air for business people being collected.

Then she saw her.

That recognisable blonde hair bouncing around her shoulders as she walked towards Nikki, suitcase pulled behind her. Jane was wearing figure-hugging jeans, and a denim jacket. Nikki's heart raced as she felt the need to run and greet Jane and bury her lips in her hair. Jane looked around her until her eyes met Nikki's, holding her gaze for what seemed like ages as she took in the rose tint on her cheeks, and wondered if this was caused by the same excitement that she felt.

Jane ran the last few paces and pulled Nikki into a bear hug. "Nikki! You look great. It's so good to see you again, I'm so grateful for you picking me up". Nikki breathed in her scent and felt her tummy stir once more.

"You're welcome and, Jane, you look fantastic. Let's get to the car and you can fill me in about what's been happening in Benidorm!"

Once inside her car, Nikki felt the closeness of Jane even more intensely as if she filled the very air she breathed and jumped a little when Jane spoke.

"So have you dealt with those demons that were keeping you awake at night?"

"Almost," Nikki said. "Well, I have served the divorce petition and Michael seems to have accepted that it's over, so that's the first step. In fact, I have to go and see him later, if you don't mind. I won't be long, and you can stay and watch TV in my room until I get back and then i will show you where you will be sleeping."

"What about your father?" asked Jane. "Won't he mind me being there without you?"

"No, he's at golf today and then having dinner with his friends. He won't be home until about 9, and I will be home long before that."

"That's cool," Jane replied. "I need to catch up on some sleep anyway. I worked until 3am this morning and haven't yet been to bed."

"Poor you! You must be exhausted. Of course, you must

sleep. I'll get you a drink and something to eat, then get your head down".

Jane covered Nikki's hand with her own as it rested on the gear stick, sending a warm feeling throughout her body.
"Thank you, Nick. You're a diamond, and I'm really glad you have things sorted. But, word of advice, be careful. Men can be very unpredictable.
"Oh I will," Nikki promised as they came to a standstill outside the house.

Stepping out of the vehicle, Jane looked at the house and whistled.
"Wow, that's some home you have there!" she turned and said to Nikki.
"Let's get inside," Nikki replied. "There's a lot about me I need to fill you in on!"

Once inside, Nikki made herself and Jane a sandwich and a coffee. Sitting together at the dining table, Nikki explained all about her life, and that her father was John Roberts – the owner of a multimillion pound property company and that she, one day, would be heiress to their fortunes and would take over the business.

After Jane digested this information, Nikki went on to explain exactly what had happened that day that had caused the break-up of her marriage.
"...So you see," Nikki finished, "The life I thought I had all

planned out – wife, mother – was all a mirage. My dreams and beliefs were left behind in tatters."

Jane was quiet for a while, absorbing everything that had just been told to her. She looked into Nikki's sad, tired eyes and hated a man she had never met for etching that pain into such a beautiful face. Moving closer to where Nikki sat, Jane spoke to her.

"You are a wonderful, beautiful woman, Nic. Don't forget we can move from one dream to another. You have a whole new chapter to write and, this time, you dictate the ending. Don't let the arrogance of that bull-headed arsehole hold you back from becoming whoever you are meant to be."

Jane ended by placing a soft kiss on Nikki's forehead. "Now you go tell him what's what!" she smiled.

Nikki returned the smile and felt those butterflies swarming around inside her.

"Let me show you to my room so you can catch up on some sleep" she said, leading the way up the stairs. "Sorry about the teenage décor!" Nikki laughed. "Not much has changed since I left home."

"I love the décor," replied Jane, joining in with Nikki's giggle.

"Well, help yourself to whatever you need," Nikki said. "I told Michael I would be there by 7:30. I really won't be that long."

"No problem, I will see you when you get back but please, Nick, be careful. Not everyone is who they seem, even if you've known them for years."

"I will," Nikki replied and as she turned to leave, Jane stopped her.

"…Hey, Nic, one more thing."

"What's that?" Nikki asked.

"Thank you for choosing the Gemelos as your retreat" Jane winked.

Nikki felt herself blush. "You're welcome," she replied as she quietly closed the door.

Jane felt the room turn colder as Nikki left. She also knew that she felt the electric charge that passed between them – what she wasn't sure of was if this was merely sexual attraction or something deeper than that. She couldn't get her out of her mind. Nikki was all she thought about and she had no intention of visiting England again until meeting Nikki.

Laying down on the bed, she breathed in deeply. She could smell Nikki upon the covers. This brought her a feeling of contentment as she closed her eyes and, with a smile on her lips, Jane drifted off to sleep. She dreamed of sharing the bed with Nikki, their bodies entwined as they became one. And she knew for sure that there was no one else.

CHAPTER 9: You Belong To Me

Apart from the porch light to her marital home, there seemed to be no other sign that anyone was at home. In fact, Nikki wondered if she had got the wrong evening. But, pulling up in the drive, she hurried over and rang the doorbell. After a few moments, she heard footsteps and the door opened just a crack.

"Michael, it's me," Nikki said.

Opening the door wider, Michael smiled.

"Right on time," he replied. "Come in. I'm in the kitchen. Would you like a coffee, or perhaps something a little stronger?" he asked.

Nikki saw the unsteadiness in his walk. "Oh, Michael, you have been drinking again? I thought I was coming here so we could discuss things sensibly."

"I've only had a couple," Michael replied as he lifted the bottle and offered Nikki a glass.

"No, thanks. Coffee will be fine," she replied as she took a seat at the table.

She felt uneasy. Every sense in her body was wary, as if she should get up and leave now, especially after what had happened last time she was here and Michael had been drinking. She thought back to where she had left Jane sleeping. That's where she wanted to be. She pictured her naked body pushed up against Jane's, the woman she wanted. Her brain suddenly froze. The woman she wanted, she thought to herself. That's who she was. She was the only person Nikki really wanted. A slight glow lit her cheeks at this revelation.

"So, how have you been Nikki?" Michael asked.

"I've been fine," Nikki replied as Michael placed a mug of coffee in front of her and took a seat opposite her.

"Well, you certainly look good," Michael continued. "You seem to have a glow about you. Reminds me of the old you before all this happened." He gestured with his hands between them both. "Me and you were so good together, Nikki. How did we ever let things get this bad between us? Nikki... Do you miss me? Do you miss us?"

"Michael, please, I haven't come here to reminisce. You asked me here to discuss the sale of the house and to settle things amicably with the divorce. I was thinking, if you want to keep the house, maybe you could buy me out. Of course, you can keep everything that's in here, and I can talk to dad about you keeping the company car," Nikki said, trying to steer the conversation away from where it seemed to be heading.

"You think your dad would agree to letting me keep anything? He hates me Nikki and you know it. He sacked me, took away a career I loved... Your suggestion, I take it?" Michael asked.

"No, not my suggestion, but you have to agree it would have been almost impossible for us to work together after all that's happened" Nikki responded.

"Not for me, Nikki" Michael replied. "We could have still worked together but obviously I am being punished for the one and only indiscretion I ever made in our marriage – everything else forgotten as if we were never together."

"Please, Michael, I don't want to rake over what's passed. I want to discuss the future, I want to move on, I want you to move on and I want to make it as easy as possible for the both of us."

"It seems as if you have already moved on," Michael replied, helping himself to another glass of whisky, his words becoming slurred. "Was I that easy to forget Nikki? Were our dreams so easy to let go of?"

Nikki looked across the table at the man she once loved, she wished more than ever that she hadn't come here this evening. She didn't like the path their conversation was taking, or the intent look in Michael's eyes, but his words fed the anger she still felt towards him.

"Was it so easy to forget we were married when you fucked my best friend?" Nikki retorted, then instantly regretted her comment when she saw the dark flush appear across Michael's face. She had made him angry.

"Look, Michael, I shouldn't have said that. It's just this is bringing back bad memories for us both. I just want us to end this as amicably as possible."

"There's just one problem with that, Nikki," Michael said, leaning closer across the table so that she could smell the alcohol on his breath, making her want to gag.

"Which is?" Nikki asked, a feeling of trepidation knotting in her stomach.

"I don't want things to end and, deep down, I don't think you want that either," Michael replied.

Nikki didn't like this Michael. The drunk, unpredictable Michael.

"I can see that you've had too much to drink this evening. Maybe we should leave talking for another day and you should get yourself some sleep." Nikki got up as she was speaking and picked up her bag. "Call me in the morning and we can arrange another time," she said as she made to go past Michael towards the door.

Michael got up from his chair and stepped in front of her, even more unsteady on his feet now but also showing a look of determination on his face.

"No, Nikki, you don't get to walk out on me a second time," he spat. Then, softening his tone, he continued. "You're upset and hurt. I understand that. But once you're carrying our child, things will get better. You will feel more secure and we can get back to how happy we used to be."

Nikki's feet seemed glued to the spot. Did he just say she was going to carry his baby? Did he honestly believe she would ever let him near her again after he had betrayed her? Finding her voice, she spoke, with as much calmness as she could.

"Michael, I am divorcing you. I will never carry your child. The drink is effecting your brain. Now, if you will excuse me, I am going home."

Michael grabbed hold of Nikki's wrist. "But, Nikki, you are home. This is what you have always wanted. A family of your own. So that's what I am going to do for you, Nikki. For us. I'm going to turn that dream into reality and everything else will fall into place… you will see."

Nikki tried to break free from his grip but he was too strong. The weight of his words bringing bile to her throat, Michael pulled her to him. "Don't fight this Nikki. We both know this is what you want."

With those final words, he crushed his lips against hers.

Jane thought the tapping on the door was part of her dream. Opening her eyes, it took her a few seconds to remember where she was. Then, the tapping came again, this time followed by a man's voice.

"Nikki, darling, are you awake?"

Jane got off the bed and opened the door, coming face to face with who she thought must be Nick's father.

"Oh, I'm sorry, you must be Jane. I'm John, Nikki's father. Is she asleep?"

"No, no, she's not here. She said she had to meet Michael to discuss things, and I fell asleep. I'm sorry, err, John, yes, I'm Jane. It's good to meet you." Jane replied.

"What time is it?" John looked at his watch, worry etched on his face. "It's 10:30… How long has she been gone?"

"A good 3 hours, and she said she would be back before you…" Jane's look of concern now matched John's.

"If that bastard has laid a hand on her, I will kill him."

"Would he lay a hand on her"? Jane asked, a knot forming in her tummy."

"He's been drinking heavily lately and who knows what he's capable of when he's drunk. I'm going to drive over there. You wait here in case she comes home."

"No, please, John, let me come with you! I need to know she's alright. Sitting here on my own, my mind will be in overdrive. If she's in trouble I want to help."

John nodded his head. "OK. Let's go and find her."

They walked to John's car in complete silence, each deep in their own thoughts and the worry for the woman they both loved showing on their faces. They took off at speed, wanting to get to the house as quickly as they could.

Nikki was in shock. She couldn't believe what was happening, but she was left in no uncertainty as to what Michael wanted to happen. She knew she had to get out of this house. She also knew that anger wouldn't help her – not with Michael behaving like this.

Think.

Think Nikki.

She needed to calm him down, to let him believe she wanted what he wanted until she figured out how to get out of here. So, forcing the bile back, she returned his kiss.

She felt Michael pause for a moment before leaning back into the kiss, his touch more tender now that she was responding. After a minute or two, Michael pulled back, and held Nikki at arm's length.

"Are you playing with me, Nikki?" he asked. "It's dangerous to play games like that."

"I'm not playing games, Michael, but can we please sit down and talk about us? That's what you want, isn't it? I know I do," Nikki lied.

Doubt flicked across Michael's face and, for a moment, Nikki thought he was going to ignore her request and carry her off to the bedroom like a caveman.

She gave him her sweetest smile.

"Please," she requested again.

Michael let go of her and gestured towards the chair she had been sitting in previously, and he sat opposite her once more.

"Michael, you think this hasn't affected me? The thought of losing you, losing our dreams, broke me," she said. "But I thought you didn't love me anymore – that's why I filed for divorce. I would never have done that if I had known you still loved me," she lied.

Michael sat quietly, watching her face intently for any sign that she may be lying, but Nikki kept her mask firmly in place.

She felt as if her whole life depended on it.

"I would love to believe the dreams we had still live inside of you, my love," she continued. "But not like this – not in anger. If we really want this to work, it has to be with love. Planning children should be a happy time, my darling, so let's do that now. Let's plan our future."

Michael stayed quiet for what seemed like ages before he spoke.

"And your father, Nikki? You think your father will be happy with that? He has tried to destroy me," he spat.

"Leave my father to me," Nikki replied. "All he's ever wanted is for me to be happy and, once he sees I am, then everything will go back to how it was... your career, us, our children," she continued. She decided to call her father to tell him the 'good news'. That would convince Michael that she wasn't lying. She knew her father was clever enough to know there was something wrong and come for her... God, she hoped so.

"Is this what you really want, my darling?" Michael asked, doubt still in his eyes. "I never meant to hurt you. I promise to make it up to you for the rest of our lives if what you're saying is true," he moved from the chair opposite Nikki to the chair at her side and took her hands.

"Look at me tell me you mean this... that you love me... and that it's all going to be OK."

Just the touch of his skin made Nikki feel nauseas. How she stopped herself from pulling her hands free, she didn't know. She just knew that she had to be allowed to use the phone, so with every bit of actress she never knew she possessed, she looked Michael in the eyes.

"I love you Michael, you have to believe me. There's nothing more I want in this life than to continue to be your wife and live the dreams we have always had."

Michael looked deeply at his wife, a slow smile appearing on his lips spreading to his eyes

"Oh, Nikki, I believe you, my darling," he said, leaning forwards, kissing her. "So, you will stay tonight," he continued. "Tonight will be the first night of the rest of our lives. We will love one another again, my darling. We shall start rebuilding our dreams tonight."

"I will stay – of course I will," Nikki said. "But I have to ring my dad and let him know where I am. He will be worried."

"No, no phone calls. You're a big girl, Nikki. You don't need your father's permission to stay with you husband."

"Not his permission, no, but he will be worried because he thinks I'm returning tonight. I don't want him driving all this way looking for me. Surely you can understand that, my love?" Nikki said, her heart racing. What if he refused? How the hell would she get out of this mess? "After all, when we have children, we would want to know they were safe, wouldn't we? He may think I've had a car crash or something."

Michael sat thinking for a while. "OK, one quick call to let him know you're ok, but I want to be there when you make the call and give him our good news."

Nikki nodded her head.

Michael took Nikki's hand. "We can use the phone in the bedroom, my love" he said.

Feeling that she had no choice but to follow him, she got up from the chair and allowed him to lead her out of the kitchen.

Chapter 10: In Janes Arms

John pulled up outside the house Nikki once shared with Michael. All the lights were off but he saw Nikki's car in the driveway and knew she was there. A feeling of fear washed over him. He knew his daughter. She wouldn't want to be here a minute longer than she had to. A Michael fuelled with alcohol may be too much for his daughter to handle. The thought of her hurt or frightened went around in his head as he stopped and got out of the car. Stepping onto the gravelled driveway, every part of him was alert for the slightest noise. Jane got out the passenger side and walked towards John.

"You stay here," John said to her. "Keep your mobile handy in case there is any trouble and, if there is, then call the police."

Jane's heart thumped against her chest, the whole place seemed eerily quiet. Pictures of a bruised, battered Nikki flashed through her mind. If he had hurt her, Jane could quite easily go to prison for what she would do to him in return, she thought. Shaking her head, trying to get rid of the images that tortured her mind, she wished they were both back in Benidorm, sipping wine in her apartment. Anywhere but here.

"Jane?" John barked "Did you hear what I said? Pull yourself together. Nikki needs us. Stay focused." Jane nodded in his direction. Seeing the fear and worry in Jane's face, John softened his voice. "Don't worry. We won't be going home without Nikki... just stay alert and keep hold of that mobile," he said, placing a comforting arm around Jane's shoulders.

Jane nodded again. "Don't worry – I won't let either of you down," she replied softly.

John smiled at Jane. "Try not to worry," he said, making his way towards the front door. Fear of what Nikki may be experiencing pulsed through his whole body.

Banging on the door, he stood tense, ears straining for the slightest noise. The door remained unanswered. This time he banged harder. "Nikki, darling, I know you're in there. Are you OK?" he called through the wooden barrier. Just then, he was sure he heard movement inside. Hammering at the door, he called out again. "Michael? Michael! I know Nikki's there. Her car's here. Open the door before I kick the thing in."

"Go home, John," Michael called back. "Nikki's fine. You have no right coming here this time of night and disturbing us. Nikki's tired. She'll be home in the morning. Leave."

As Michael shouted the words in the direction of the front door, he had his hand placed tightly over Nikki's mouth, holding her firmly against him so that she couldn't call out.

"Tell Nikki to tell me that," John growled. "Bring her to the door."

Michael, with his free hand, put a finger to his lips, warning Nikki to keep quiet. "What do you think I have done to her, John? I'm her husband and if I tell you she's tired, then she's tired. We've worked things out. We're back together. That's all you need to know. Go home."

"Nikki!" John started to shout louder. "Nick? Can you hear me? Are you OK? Has that bastard hurt you?" he shouted, ignoring whatever Michael was telling him, knowing that if she was able to, she would have opened the door to him by now.

"What you going to do John? Take everything away from me? You've done that, but Nikki is one thing you're not taking. We're going to have a baby. You can kiss any chance you have of seeing your grandchild goodbye. Now go home, and let us get on with making our family. Do you hear me John? Michael screamed through the door. "I said, do you hear me?"

John's blood ran cold. Grandchild? What the hell was he doing to her in there? He knew Nikki had no intention of getting back with Michael, let alone having his child. John decided to change tactics.

Quieting his tone, John called through the locked door. "Look, Michael, I know deep-down you're a good guy. You have been through a lot. Open the door. Let's talk man to man. Let me see Nick and, if this is what she wants, I will walk away." While talking, John motioned for Jane to call the police. Michael obviously thought he had nothing left to lose, but John was not going to lose his daughter.

Jane made the call. Fingers trembling, she relayed to the emergency responder what was happening, and begged the police to come quickly. The lady on the other end of the phone assured Jane that they were on their way. Jane gave a thumbs-up sign to John.

"Now you want to talk?" came Michael's reply. "I thought you had done talking with me when you fired me – when you threatened to leave me with nothing – but you were wrong, John. I have not been left with nothing. I have Nikki and she's going to have my baby."

Every muscle in John's body ached with the effort of trying to keep calm. He wanted to smash his way into that house and shake Michael by the neck, but he knew he had to tread carefully. He didn't know what state Nikki was in and any show of aggression could impact on her safety.

"Maybe you are right, Michael. Maybe I was too rash... too harsh to you on that day. I'm a father and, seeing my little girl hurt, I lashed out without thinking. If Nikki is happy, then I'm happy. I'm sure we can sort this. Your job is still open, and if you're going to be having a family, maybe a promotion? Babies don't come cheap," John chuckled, trying to sound calm and sincere.

All went quiet for a while and, for a moment, John thought that Michael wasn't going to reply. If only he knew where Nikki was right now… if she was OK…

Suddenly, Michael's reply broke his trail of thought. "I don't believe you. You just want me to open the door, so you can persuade Nikki to leave me."

John could hear that Michael's words were becoming more slurred, fuelled with alcohol and, in this frame of mind, God knows what he was capable of. John had to get him to open that door. He tried again.

"Nikki's with you, isn't she?" John said. "You must have discussed all of this, if you've decided to get back together and start a family, she must be happy, or she wouldn't still be here, would she? So if Nikki's happy, then I'm happy, Michael. You must know that all I want is for my daughter to be happy."

From the other side of the door, Michael looked at Nikki. "Are you happy, Nikki?" he asked. Nikki nodded her head and made sure that her eyes didn't betray her. She never knew she was such a good actress. Michael looked at her intently, studying every feature, then looked deeply into her eyes and slowly smiled. He saw love and tenderness in those eyes. "Oh, Nikki, we are going to be so happy" he said, still unsure whether John was lying or if he was really going to gain back everything just for making Nikki happy.

"If I open the door, you'll try to push your way in and ruin everything," Michael called out.

John could hear that Michael was wavering. He tried again. "No! No, I won't, Michael. I just want to put things right, like you and Nikki have. I want to be part of your lives, whatever the cost. You don't even have to let me in… just let me see Nick and then maybe we could talk tomorrow, after a good night's sleep… and we can put all this behind us."

"If I open the door and Nikki tells you she's OK, and that she's happy, you will go home?" Michael asked.

"Yes, I will go home. I just want to see Nikki and then, tomorrow, you come into the office… we will discuss your promotion… new office… new car… get things back on track."

Michael was liking what he was hearing: a new position within the company, with a big office and fancy car, setting him up for his next big promotion when the old man died or retired. He would take over the company, and then he would be complete. No one to tell him what to do… he would have it all, and Nikki safe at home with their children, showing him the respect he deserved as her husband.

John held his breath and prayed that Michael was drunk enough and stupid enough to believe him.

Michael slid open the bolts and turned the key in the lock.

Upon hearing this, John's body was poised; ready to pounce at any minute. But, as the door opened, he had to take a step back. Standing in front of him was Nikki, Michael close behind, with one arm looped over her shoulder, presenting a picture of togetherness. But Nikki's eyes belied the image, for John saw fear in them. His blood boiled as he took in the paleness of his daughter's skin and the look in her eyes. He wanted to pull her out the doorway into his arms where he could keep her safe forever, but he also knew that any sudden movement or aggression would result in the door being slammed shut again, and he didn't want Nikki getting hurt in any scuffle.

"Nikki, darling, I was so worried about you. You should have called to say you were staying here." John directed the conversation towards his daughter in a calm tone but his eyes relayed that he knew she wasn't here at her own free will.

"I'm… I'm sorry, dad," Nikki stuttered. "I didn't mean to worry you. I was just about to call when you arrived. Isn't it great news that Michael and I are getting back together?" she gushed. "He was just about to take me upstairs as he feels that a family will bring us closer together," she continued.

John wasn't silly. He listened intently to every word… *he* was about to take me upstairs… *he* felt a family would bring them closer together… what the hell was Michael going to force Nikki to do for God's sake?

"I understand exactly what you're telling me, my darling," John replied, now turning his attention to Michael himself. "I'm so happy for you both," he lied. "You have made my day, seeing my daughter so happy again. Let's shake hands on the future and put the past behind us," John said, offering an outstretched hand.

Although Michael's demeanour had relaxed a little at hearing his wife confirm that they were back together, John saw a look of mistrust flicker across Michael's face, so he continued. "After all, we will have a lot to discuss about your new position when you return to work on Monday".

Michael took this in and relaxed even further, extending his hand to receive John's. At that moment, the police headlights shone into the driveway. Before Michael could react, Nikki's father grabbed the the outstretched hand and pulled Michael out of the house, the sudden movement unsteadying them both as they fell to the ground.

"Run to the car!" John called out to his daughter. She did as she was told, running as fast as her feet would carry her – and that's when she saw Jane.

Jane stood there with open arms. Nikki ran straight into her embrace. "You're safe now, darling," Jane soothed.

"Get that bastard away from my daughter and keep him away, or by God, I will," John shouted at the two officers, one of which was handcuffing Michael and the other preparing to do the same to John.

"No! No!" Nikki cried, running towards her father. "He has done nothing wrong! My dad was protecting me," she directed at the police officers.

"Calm down," one of the officers replied. "This is just procedure. We found both men fighting and are now taking them to the police station where statements can be made as to what has occurred. You should come as well to give your version of events, please."

"But I'm telling you… my father has done nothing wrong," Nikki continued.

"If that's the case, the sooner we get you all to the station, the sooner we can release him."

"Nik, darling," John said. "I'm fine. What about you? Are you hurt? Did that bastard hurt you?"

Nikki shook her head and, with tears in her eyes, continued. "But you had not arrived when you did, only God knows what would have happened." Jane placed an arm around Nikki and pulled her close. She could feel the shock of what she had been through starting to take hold as she felt Nik start to tremble in her arms.

"Is it OK to follow you guys to the station?" Jane asked the officers. "I'm sure that we all want to get this sorted as quickly as possible, so that Nikki can go home with her father, and that man," she spat looking over at Michael, "can be kept from going near her ever again".

The police nodded in response and walked both men towards the squad car.

"Nikki, baby, please. What's going on? Tell these people I'm your husband and that we love each other," Michael called out as he was being led away.

Nikki stopped in her tracks and, facing her husband, she spoke in a voice dripping with venom. "You make my skin crawl, Michael. I was never coming back to you and the thought of bearing your child makes me physically sick. You thought by locking me in and forcing what you wanted onto me it would bring back my love for you. Well, that love died the moment you fucked my best friend. There's only one person's arms I want to be in," she continued as she walked over to Jane and kissed her tenderly on the lips, "and they are not yours."

Seeing the look of confusion and anger on Michael's face as he took in what she was saying brought her some comfort. "But you belong to me, Nikki," Michael called out to her, as the police officer opened the squad car door and gestured for Michael to climb inside.

"I don't belong to you Michael," Nikki shouted back. "I belong in the arms of the woman I love, You turn my stomach and I never want to see or hear from you again."

With those parting words, Nikki and Jane walked hand in hand towards her father's car. The Nightmare finally over .... or was it?

Printed in Poland
by Amazon Fulfillment
Poland Sp. z o.o., Wrocław